HIPPOLYTA
AND THE
CURSE
OF THE
AMAZONS

Young Heroes series
Odysseus in the Serpent Maze

By Jane Yolen
The Dragon's Boy

YOUNG HEROES

HIPPOLYTA
AND THE
CURSE
OF THE
AMAZONS

By
JANE YOLEN
and
ROBERT J. HARRIS

■ HarperCollins*Publishers*

Hippolyta and the Curse of the Amazons
Copyright © 2002 by Jane Yolen and Robert J. Harris
All rights reserved. No part of this book may be used or reproduced in any manner
whatsoever without written permission except in the case of brief quotations embodied
in critical articles and reviews. Printed in the United States of America. For information
address HarperCollins Children's Books, a division of HarperCollins Publishers,
1350 Avenue of the Americas, New York, NY 10019.
www.harperchildrens.com

Library of Congress Cataloging-in-Publication Data
Yolen, Jane.
Hippolyta and the curse of the Amazons / by Jane Yolen and Robert J. Harris.
      p.   cm. — (Young heroes ; bk. 2)
Summary: Thirteen-year-old Hippolyta, a princess of the Amazons, fights to save her people
from destruction when her mother the Queen refuses to sacrifice her second-born male child.
ISBN 0-06-028736-5 — ISBN 0-06-028737-3 (lib. bdg.)
1. Hippolyta (Greek mythology)—Juvenile fiction. [1. Hippolyta (Greek mythology)—
Fiction.]   I. Harris, Robert J., 1955–   II. Title.   III. Series.
PZ7.Y78 Hmk   2002   2001024017
[Fic]—dc21   CIP
                                                                                                    AC

Typography by Carla Weise
1   2   3   4   5   6   7   8   9   10
❖
First Edition

For my young Amazons:
Lexi Callan-Piatt
Maddison Jane Piatt
Alison Isabelle Stemple
—J.Y.

To my parents:
who let me have adventures
—R.J.H.

Contents

CHAPTER ONE

DUEL

Hippolyta's eyes were fixed on the bird as it flew over the treetops. Carefully she drew an arrow from the quiver that hung at her hip, but she didn't raise her bow.

"Are you going to shoot?" asked a puzzled voice at her side.

Hippolyta shook her head irritably, jabbing an elbow at her little sister to make her move away.

Antiope took a small step backward. "The bird will be past soon."

"It's a big plump partridge," Hippolyta whispered. "It doesn't fly that fast. Besides, they're usually in pairs. Like Amazons." Antiope giggled.

"Be quiet, little one," Hippolyta said, fitting the arrow

into her bowstring. "I'm paired with you today because Mother insisted. So close your mouth and watch. It's the only way you'll learn anything."

There were a few moments of silence. Then Antiope asked again, "Shouldn't you be taking aim?"

Hippolyta lowered the bow and arrow, turned, and glared at her sister. "I *was* taking aim," she told Antiope. "One must aim with the eye, not the bow." Already she'd decided at the exact point she would fire. She'd fixed upon a spot directly ahead of the bird. But now, with Antiope's interruptions, the bird had disappeared, landing somewhere in the twisty undergrowth.

"Oh." The little girl was clearly disappointed. "It's gone."

"Never mind," Hippolyta began, then stopped speaking as the second bird took to the air.

In one quick movement Hippolyta lifted the bow, hauled back on the string, fired the arrow. The gray-brown bird flew straight into the arrow's path, and the sharpened bronze point thudded into its breast.

"By the moon!" Hippolyta gasped, for a second arrow struck the bird no more than the blink of an eye after the first. It tore through one of the outstretched wings and threw the partridge into a wild spin. The little bird plummeted to earth in a whirl of feathers right into a small copse of trees.

"What happened?" Antiope cried.

"Someone's trying to steal our dinner!" Hippolyta's

eyes narrowed angrily. Slinging her bow over her shoulder and snatching up a spear from the ground where she'd jammed it point first, Hippolyta bounded toward the copse.

"Wait for me!" Antiope squealed, running after her sister and waving her own spear, which was so small it was scarcely more than a toy. But then she was only eight years old.

Like the other Amazons, Hippolyta had been trained as a huntress from early childhood, and she knew where to search for the fallen bird. Slinging her bow over her shoulder, she raced through the undergrowth at full speed, heading toward the copse and into a small clearing. She was unpleasantly surprised to see another Amazon there before her, already tying a cord around the dead partridge's neck.

Molpadia!

No mistaking that thick tangle of yellow hair tied up in a cluster of tight braids. No mistaking that superior sneer.

"You're too slow, Hippolyta," Molpadia said. "The goddess of the hunt grants no second chances."

Molpadia was not much older than Hippolyta—less than two years—but already she wore the small square ear pendant that showed she'd killed a man in battle. Under her chin was a livid scar, a reminder of how close she'd come to dying in that same battle, when a Lycian charioteer had caught her with a stroke of his spear.

Hippolyta was tired of hearing the story. Molpadia told it at every festival. Still, earning an earbob was no excuse for taking another hunter's prize.

"You know the laws against theft," Hippolyta said, keeping her voice smooth. "It applies just as much here on the hunting grounds as it does back in Themiscyra."

"Can you deny you saw my arrow strike the bird?" Molpadia asked defiantly, lifting her chin so the scar seemed to grin.

"It was my shot that struck first. My shot that hit the breast. My shot that killed it." Hippolyta knew she could play the defiance game as well as the older girl.

"I was here first to claim the prize," Molpadia said.

Hippolyta gripped the spear in both hands, pointing the tip at Molpadia. "Claiming and keeping are two different things."

Molpadia let the partridge drop and raised her own spear. "Your mother may be one of our queens, Hippolyta, but that gives you no special status."

"I claim none," Hippolyta answered quickly, "only what is mine by right of my own arm."

"Then show me that arm," Molpadia cried, shaking off her bow and tossing aside the quiver.

It was an unmistakable call to duel. Hippolyta likewise took off bow and quiver and dropped her fur cap onto the ground. Then she began a low circle to her left.

Molpadia too began circling, and they each looked for an opening where they could strike.

Just then Antiope darted into the clearing, gasping.

Hippolyta heard her little sister but ignored everything but the older girl and the spear. Never having been in an actual battle, Hippolyta was at a slight disadvantage against Molpadia. But she'd never been wounded, either, and that gave her an edge. "Once slashed, twice shy," the Amazons said. Of course they said it of their enemies, not themselves.

Well, at this moment Molpadia *was* the enemy. Hippolyta stopped thinking and let the years of training take over.

She noticed a splash of crimson on the tip of Molpadia's spear. *The blood of my partridge*, she thought. But no, there was too much blood for such a small target.

Almost casually Hippolyta said, "Fighting already today?" She smiled and gestured with her head at the weapon. "They say the ones who fight too often are the ones who die too soon." Her battle teacher, Old Okyale, always said: "Cite laws at the foe, even if you make them up on the spot. It throws the enemy off guard."

Molpadia laughed. "I have the same teacher as you, Hippolyta. You won't catch me that way."

"But your spear is red," Hippolyta said in that same calm tone. "Either you were fighting today or you're careless with your weapons."

This time the insult struck home.

"I was tracking a mountain cat and wounded it."

"You have a habit of wounding," Hippolyta said. "Without killing."

"*You* will not be so lucky," Molpadia responded, hefting her spear a bit higher.

"Ah, but you know Amazon duels are fought only till first blood is drawn." Hippolyta noticed now that Molpadia led with her left shoulder low. That meant her right would be high and exposed.

"There's no rule about how much blood . . ." Molpadia's threat was real. "Remember that while you still have time to concede."

"An Amazon princess does not concede anything," Hippolyta said. She squinted against the sun.

"I knew you'd throw your rank in my face," Molpadia said, leading again with her left shoulder.

Antiope approached them, hands upraised. "Can't you two just share the bird?"

"That would settle nothing." Hippolyta's voice suddenly deepened. "Get out of the way, Antiope." She never took her eyes off her opponent.

At that instant Molpadia made a jab. But ready for it, Hippolyta knocked her point aside with the haft of her own spear. Before there was time for a counterattack, Molpadia jumped back out of range.

Antiope had retreated a few feet, but now she returned, as if to protect her sister. Hippolyta spotted her out of the corner of an eye. "Go! You distract me. Tend my horse, Antiope." She didn't mention that

Antiope too might be in danger should the fight get out of hand. She wondered briefly where Molpadia's pair Amazon might be.

Antiope refused to budge. "I'm going to watch," she insisted. "Watch and learn, you said."

Molpadia suddenly attacked again, and the shafts of the two spears cracked against each other several times before the two girls became locked together, neither one giving ground. But Molpadia was older and bigger and stronger, and gradually she forced her spear point down toward Hippolyta's face.

If she bloods me, I will not cry out, Hippolyta told herself. *I will not.* She could feel the heat of Molpadia's breath on her brow.

All of a sudden Hippolyta shifted her weight, throwing her opponent off-balance. She took a chance and whipped the butt of her spear up to give the older girl a crack on the head.

Molpadia reeled back with a curse, but before Hippolyta could follow up with the spearpoint, Antiope let out a shrill, awful scream.

Hippolyta twisted around and saw a mountain cat emerging from the undergrowth, a great bloody slash on its right flank still oozing blood. Its eyes were fixed on Antiope, and a vicious growl rumbled in its throat.

Antiope didn't shrink before the great cat, but her little spear was shaking in her hands. The animal was bigger than she, and only a few short yards separated them.

Hippolyta realized that the wounded cat must be crazed with pain. It was ready to spring.

As the cat leaped, Hippolyta threw herself forward, knocking Antiope off her feet. Thrusting her spear upward, Hippolyta rammed the point deep into the animal's tawny breast.

Hot blood showered down, nearly blinding her, and instinctively she pushed the spear and cat away, to keep the flailing claws from raking her face.

The cat thudded onto its side, a low growl rattled in its throat, and then it was dead.

Molpadia pointed at a wound in the cat's flank. "I did that."

"Yes, but you didn't finish the job, Molpadia. You were too slow," Hippolyta said, standing. She was amazed that her legs could still hold her, for now that the danger was passed, they were suddenly shaking with terror. She ignored her trembling legs and wrenched the spear from the cat's body.

Taking a deep breath, she hefted the cat onto her shoulders, caring nothing for the blood that trickled down her arm. The golden hide would make a fine tunic or a warm lining for a winter cloak. The cat's teeth she'd turn into a necklace for Antiope, who had stood so bravely, armed only with her little toy spear.

"Keep the bird, Molpadia," Hippolyta said with a grin of triumph. "I have a better prize now." She handed her spear to Antiope. "Here, sister, if you carry this for me, we'll head for home. Two hunters together."

Antiope took the spear, and it was so much larger than her own she had to wrap both arms around it. But she didn't complain. Her grin practically swallowed her face.

Molpadia followed silently behind, the partridge slung over her shoulder.

They were within sight of the tethered mare when another horse came galloping through the trees.

Molpadia had already snatched up her bow and arrow, ready to fire, but the rider was no enemy from Phrygia or Lycia. It was Aella, one of the queen's royal guards.

"Hippolyta, thank the goddess I have found you," Aella called, waving an arm. "You and Antiope must return at once to the palace."

"What is it? What has happened?" Hippolyta cried out.

But message delivered, Aella had already turned and was riding back the way she'd come.

Antiope stood trembling, arms around the spear. "Is Mother all right, Hippolyta? Is—"

Without answering, Hippolyta threw the cat to the ground. She grabbed the spear from her little sister, then dragged her to the horse. Untying the mount, Hippolyta leaped onto its bare back, then leaned down. "To me!" she cried.

Antiope reached up and was yanked onto the horse's

back, behind Hippolyta. Fastening her arms around her sister's waist, she nestled her head into the small of Hippolyta's back.

"Ready," she cried.

Then they were off at a gallop toward Themiscyra, the royal capital, as fast as their hardy little mountain pony could go.

CHAPTER TWO

THE QUEEN

ll Hippolyta could see of Aella was the dust her horse had kicked up speeding back home.

She turned and looked behind her. Almost at the edge of sight were Molpadia and, farther behind her, another figure, presumably the girl Molpadia had been hunting with.

"Will we get there soon? Will Mother be all right? Will . . ." Antiope's questions filled Hippolyta's ears.

"I know nothing," Hippolyta called over her shoulder. "No more than you do. Now be quiet."

Soon the gleam of the River Thermodon was visible ahead, like a long, shiny-skinned adder winding its way north to the dark waters of the Euxine Sea.

On the banks of the river stood the capital of Themiscyra, a quiet settlement of wooden lodges, cabins, and storehouses that had the slightly ramshackle air of a temporary encampment. Hippolyta knew that long ago the Amazons, like their Scythian ancestors, had traveled from place to place, living off the land. But finally they had settled here, close to the running waters.

To Hippolyta, however, Themiscyra was home, the only place she wanted to be.

As soon as she and Antiope dismounted and led the pony through the gate of the wooden palisade and past a row of merchants' stalls, she could hear the buzz of voices filling the street. It was not the usual, happy sound of women at work. Hippolyta was sure it was like the sharp *pick-buzz* of angry insects. She couldn't quite make out what people were saying.

About halfway into the city, they came upon a knot of women debating vigorously and clogging the way.

"Not another?" one gray-haired merchant was saying.

"It's the will of Artemis," answered another.

"What's to be done? What's to be done?" The same question was suddenly in a dozen mouths.

"The queen will know" came the answer from a weaver, her hands full of cloth. "She will do what is right."

"What is right? Or what is best?" That was the merchant.

"I trust the queen," the weaver said again.

Hippolyta pushed them aside. "Let us through."

But when the merchant cried to her, "What says Queen Otrere, princess? What says your mother?" Hippolyta glared at her.

"We know nothing," she answered. "Nor can we find out if you don't let us go to her."

Silently the women made a path for the two girls, and about fifty feet farther in, they reached the courtyard of the royal palace.

Like the other buildings, it was built of wood but reinforced with slate and sandstone. Normally Hippolyta's heart lifted whenever she came home. But this time it was as if a heavy gray mist hung over the turreted roof.

Hippolyta gratefully handed a servant girl the pony's reins, and her weapons as well. Then she and Antiope went over to Aella. "What is it?" Hippolyta asked. "What's happened?"

"Hush," Aella said. "We can't speak of it here. Inside, quickly. But don't run. Walk like princesses. Like Amazons. Heads high. Show no fear. You are daughters of Otrere."

Hippolyta squared her shoulders and saw out of the corner of her eye that her little sister did the same. Then, following Aella, they went into the palace, into a danger they did not yet understand.

The mood inside the palace was subdued, as if everyone was afraid to speak openly. Aella led them straight to the queen's bedchamber. A pair of armed guards, black hair bound up in warrior's knots, flanked the closed door.

"Asteria? Philippis?" Antiope said, but they didn't answer, and that was odd because she was a great favorite with the guards.

"Come," Hippolyta said, taking her by the hand.

Silently the guards opened the doors, and they went in.

Queen Otrere was propped up in her bed. The old priestess Demonassa, who also acted as a midwife, was standing at the bedside in long gray robes that were now stained with birth blood. Seated at the bed foot was Hippolyta's younger sister Melanippe, who was just two years older than little Antiope.

Melanippe looked up and sighed. "Thank the goddess you're here, sisters." She stood and came over to them. "When I sent for Orithya, she refused to come."

"*Orithya.*" Hippolyta spoke her older sister's name as if it burned her mouth. These days Orithya spent more time with the warrior queen Valasca, who commanded the army in times of war, than she did with her own mother. Hippolyta was furious with Orithya. Family should come first.

"That Orithya would not answer your call is no surprise." Hippolyta added, "I no longer consider her a sister. The blood runs thin in her. She belongs to Valasca just as if she came shooting out between that old hawk's legs fully armored."

Antiope spotted her mother and saw what she was holding in her arms—unbound and naked. Rushing forward with a great grin, Antiope cried out, "The baby! She's here at last."

"The baby," Hippolyta said, looking over at the bed. Suddenly she realized what all the people outside had been talking about. The child hadn't been swaddled yet, and even from this far away, she could see it was a boy, the second such her mother had borne. The first had been nine years earlier, right after Melanippe, a year before Antiope.

Hippolyta remembered that day well. She'd been four years old, which was old enough to love the infant and old enough to understand that it could never remain in Themiscyra. Boys were not welcome in Amazon society, and they were given away to passing strangers. Except for the firstborn boy born to a queen: He was always returned to his father.

But not the second.

Hippolyta knew Amazon history. Every girl her age

was well versed in it: Long ago in the city of Arimaspa, the Amazon women had been part of the Scythian race. They'd lived with men and cared for their sons. But a pair of arrogant princes had brought ruin to the people by stealing gold belonging to the gods. In turn the gods rained destruction down on Arimaspa.

The goddess Artemis had saved them, leading the women away from that cursed place one moonless night. They spent years looking for the right place to establish a community of women, free of all kings, princes, and husbands, a community dedicated to the goddess.

Artemis decreed that all sons born to the women from then on were to be sent away before their first birthdays. However, there was a special rule for the Amazon queens. They would be allowed only one live son, for it had been foretold by Artemis' brother, the god Apollo, that if a second son born to a queen were allowed to grow to manhood, he would be the cause of the death of the Amazon race. It was why the priestesses and midwives supplied the queens with special herbs and potions that almost always guaranteed a girl child.

Almost.

But not always.

Antiope was playing with the baby's little fingers and singing softly to him, oblivious.

"You know what this means?" Melanippe whispered, twisting a finger through her brown curls.

Hippolyta nodded. Then she went over to the bed and took her mother's weakly offered hand. "I'm so sorry, Mother," she said, her voice tearing as if on a splinter of wood. "I know how hard this will be on you."

There was a spark of determination in Otrere's eyes, a spark that lent strength to her pale face. Her voice was amazingly firm. "I can't do what is expected, Hippolyta," she said. "Not having carried this child below my heart. You must be prepared for the worst."

Confused, Hippolyta let her mother's hand drop. "I don't understand. What do you mean, you *can't* do it? Artemis requires it. A second son *must* be sacrificed upon Artemis' altar. It's the price we pay for the goddess's protection. It's our pact with her. In this life an Amazon does what she must. How often have you told me so?"

For a moment Otrere's face went pale. Old Demonassa started forward, but the queen sat up, color rushing back into her cheeks. She waved Demonassa away.

"I can't sacrifice the child, daughter. I have felt him like a hammer beneath my breast," Otrere said. "He kicked with such life. I cannot believe the goddess would have me snuff out such a fighter."

"But—" Hippolyta took a deep breath and tried to frame her response carefully. She might not get another chance. "If you *don't* do this thing, there will be awful consequences. To you. To the child. To *all* your children." She waved her hand around the room, taking in her sisters as well as the guards and the priestess.

For a moment Otrere glanced down at the little boy in her arms, and her brown eyes filled with tears. Then she looked up again. "I don't know how to answer you, my dearest daughter. That is why I wanted you here as soon as possible. Before word spreads."

"Then you shouldn't have sent me away yesterday to teach your littlest daughter to hunt," Hippolyta answered her bitterly. "It's already too late to stop this news from reaching your people."

Just then the door to the bedchamber flew open, and a dozen warriors filed in, led by the hawk-faced Valasca. They were in full armor, shields, and helmets, and the noise they made marching into the chamber was deafening.

Valasca's bronze helmet cast deep shadows over her face, emphasizing the sharpness of her cheekbones and nose. A Gorgon's head decorated her shield. She looked as fierce as any goddess.

The infant started crying, a thin, high-pitched wail.

Hippolyta felt something cold settle in her stomach. But when she saw her sister Orithya in the second row of the troop of warriors, as well as a smirking Molpadia standing in the back of the group, her cheeks got hot with anger.

Halting at the bed foot, the battle queen slowly removed her helmet. Her black hair was caught up in a warrior's knot. She stared down at the naked infant. "A boy," she said, making it sound like a sentence of death. Which it was.

Looking accusingly at Demonassa, Valasca let her right hand rest lightly on the double-headed ax that hung from her belt. It was a threat, and it worked. Old Demonassa stepped back but did not lower her eyes.

"Did the omens give no warnings?" Valasca said in a cool voice.

The old woman shrugged. "The omens were obscure."

As usual, thought Hippolyta.

"I thought you had more magic than that," Valasca said.

"I saved my magic to ease the birth and deliver the child safely," the old woman answered.

"You needn't have bothered," Valasca said.

On the bed Otrere drew the baby closer to her breast. "What the Fates decide cannot be undone."

"No, Otrere, you mistake it. This is quite easily undone," Valasca answered in her cold voice. "A cloth over the child's face. A knife across its throat. You know the laws, Otrere, and they bind our queens even more than they bind the rest of our race."

Otrere bent her head, but whether in obeisance to her fellow queen or to look at the child again, Hippolyta couldn't have said.

"A queen," Valasca continued, her voice filling the room, "may bear only one live son. If the second grows up, he will bring about the destruction of our race. I know it, you know it. By the goddess, we *all* know it. Let this child live, and we break the pact made with Artemis by all the mothers before us. The goddess has not protected us all these years so we can be destroyed by one boy child!"

Otrere didn't answer, but a single tear escaped her right eye. Hippolyta longed to wipe it away before it shamed them all.

"You and the priestess did not take the easier way, so now you must sacrifice this child with your own knife upon the altar of Artemis," Valasca said. "Such is our law. The goddess has willed it."

"I cannot." Otrere's voice was low but adamant.

"Then you must give up your throne, and another will perform the sacrifice," Valasca said. "Either way, Otrere, the boy dies."

Otrere looked up, her eyes now clear of tears. "We all must die, Valasca. But this child is innocent of any wrongdoing. Only I, who desired one last child before I could have no more, am to blame." She sat up straighter and looked slowly around the room as if addressing every woman there. "The child can be returned to his father. Like his brother before him. If anyone is to be sacrificed, let it be me."

"Mother, no!" Melanippe and Antiope cried out together.

Hippolyta found she couldn't speak. It was as if a spell of silence had been placed upon her tongue.

Valasca shook her head. "You know that can't be, Otrere. The pact says that the babe is to be sacrificed, not the mother. Killing you—much as I might enjoy it—will not save us from the goddess's will." She signaled two of her older warriors. "Take the boy."

Otrere enveloped the baby in her arms and turned away.

Suddenly, without thinking, Hippolyta found herself moving forward and blocking the two warriors before they could reach the bed. She held her hunting knife chest high, ready to strike.

"Otrere is still your queen," she told them sharply. "Not Valasca, who rules only in times of war. You will not lay hands on Otrere."

"Step aside, Hippolyta," warned a familiar voice.

Hippolyta looked toward the speaker and saw that Molpadia had drawn her bow and it was aimed right at her heart. At this distance Molpadia could not possibly miss.

All at once the baby started to cry again, a thin, mewling sound.

Hippolyta could see her older sister, Orithya, behind Molpadia, looking helplessly from one queen to the other, torn between the oath that bound her to Valasca and the blood that bound her to Otrere. Shaking her head, Orithya suddenly strode forward and shoved the point of Molpadia's arrow aside.

"Do you plan to defile the royal bedchamber with blood?" she demanded, voice shaking. "How is that the will of the gods?"

"The will of the gods is that we obey our own laws." Valasca gave the answer in her stone voice, never taking her eyes from Otrere. "And we will spill blood, even here, to obey them."

"There'll be no killing in this place," Demonassa declared, stepping forward to stand by Hippolyta's side. "That would surely anger Artemis more than anything." At her voice, everyone but Queen Otrere looked at her. "But the child's sacrifice can only be accomplished when the moon is half in shadow, half in light, poised between life and death. And that will not be for ten days yet. Surely you know that, Valasca, who knows the rules so well."

Valasca's face grew even sharper, if that were possible. She looked, Hippolyta thought, quite a bit like her own ax.

"I will take the child and keep him quiet," Demonassa said, adding, "You will want him alive on the altar, or the sacrifice will be worth nothing."

Otrere gave up the child readily enough to the old priestess.

Valasca said softly, "By your own wish you are queen no longer. Another will perform the sacrifice. You will remain here for the ten days with only a single attendant to care for you. After that, you shall be brought for judgment before the court of the Nines."

Demonassa wrapped the child lightly in soft deerskin and walked out of the room, accompanied by Valasca and her guards.

Hippolyta and her sisters followed reluctantly behind, but Hippolyta was thinking: *That gives us ten days, thanks to Demonassa.*

But then she quickly wondered: *Ten days to do what?*

CHAPTER THREE

THE PRISONER

Because her mother was no longer queen, Hippolyta had to leave the palace where she'd lived all her life and move into the warriors' communal barracks. It was more a jolt to her heart than her body. After all, none of the Amazons led pampered lives. Even the queens were trained as hunters and farmers.

Hippolyta had looked forward to joining the ranks of the warriors in two years, when she entered her fifteenth year and had gone on her Long Mission, trekking into the wilderness for a month on her own. Now she was there sooner than anyone had planned.

Being escorted by armed guards to the barracks like a prisoner, being forcibly separated from her younger sisters, made Hippolyta furious. After all, even if their mother had broken a law, *they* had done nothing wrong. But Valasca had insisted that they be guarded in case they tried to do something foolish. Like help their mother escape.

"At least," Hippolyta pleaded with two of the warriors set over her as guards, "let me see how Antiope and Melanippe are doing."

"They are Amazons," said one frostily.

"They will be fine," the other added, though she at least smiled down at Hippolyta.

"*They* are little girls," Hippolyta answered angrily. "And if they have to be apart from their mother, at least—"

"Antiope and Melanippe are in the Halls of Athena," the frosty guard replied, "dwelling along with other girls whose mothers have died, in sickness or in battle."

"Our mother hasn't died," Hippolyta said through gritted teeth.

"Not yet" came the icy reply.

Hippolyta drew in a sharp breath.

The other guard put her hand on Hippolyta's and said softly, "I'll see what I can do."

It took five days before Hippolyta was allowed a short visit with her sisters, accompanied by two guards.

The Halls of Athena was really one large lodge with two wings sitting atop a rise. The girls lived in the smaller wing, in separate rooms.

Hippolyta visited with Melanippe first and found that she'd adjusted well to her new surroundings.

"Antiope does nothing but cry," Melanippe said. "I can't seem to help her. The other girls are mean to us, of course. But they take their lead from the matrons here, who say that Mother intended the Amazon race to die." She looked grim. "It's not true, is it?"

"Of course it's not true. Mother doesn't want anyone to die. Not even the baby."

"I *knew* it!" Melanippe said. Relief suffused her face.

"Be strong." Hippolyta gave her sister a quick hug, stood, and went across the hallway to Antiope's room.

Antiope was sitting all alone on a narrow bed, staring out the window and across the top of the palisade to where the black waters of the Euxine Sea lay along the horizon.

"Antiope?" Hippolyta called, but the little girl didn't seem to hear. "*Antiope.*"

This time Antiope turned and stared at Hippolyta, tears coursing down her cheeks.

In two long steps Hippolyta was across the room and onto the bed, wrapping her arms around her little sister. "There, there," she said, sounding exactly like their mother.

"What—" Antiope gulped, started again. "What's the baby done that's so wrong?" She swiped at her brimming eyes with the backs of her hands.

"It's not that he's done anything wrong," Hippolyta whispered into her sister's hair. "It's just that he's a male, and it's our law."

"I hate our law then," Antiope cried. "I wish somebody would take it away and burn it!"

Trying not to smile, Hippolyta sat back and looked into Antiope's dark eyes. "Without laws, sister, there would be no Themiscyra. No Long Mission. No—"

"Then I guess I don't hate *all* of it," Antiope said. She bit her lower lip. "Just the dead baby part."

Hippolyta nodded. "I hate that part too. But it *is* the law." Then she embraced her sister again, stood, and was gone.

The next day Hippolyta heard that Otrere had been moved from the palace into the prison by the palisade where criminals were commonly kept. The rumor was that Valasca was trying to starve her into submission.

Or just starve her, Hippolyta thought. *Then Valasca could proclaim herself queen of both war and peace.* She wondered which lawbreaking was worse, her mother's or the warrior queen's.

For several days Hippolyta attempted to visit her mother. She argued with the two guards at the barracks about it until she wore them down. But the prison guards were of sterner stuff. They turned her back roughly, as if they'd no idea who she was.

"Orders are that no one gets in to see the old queen," they said.

"You can't treat me this way," Hippolyta yelled at them. "I'm her daughter!"

They laughed.

"She prefers sons," said one.

It was the laughter, not the rough handling, that hurt. Hippolyta stormed off toward the drill field, her two barracks guards in tow. They watched as she crossed the field to face her older sister, who was working out with her sword.

"Have you heard what's happening to Mother?" Hippolyta demanded, grabbing Orithya by the sword arm. "She's locked up as a prisoner."

Orithya shook Hippolyta off and wiped her sweaty face with the back of her arm. Her copper hair was braided tightly behind her, but there were little sweaty wisps around her temples. "Otrere brought it on herself by her own stubbornness."

"How can you be so hard-hearted? She's our *mother!*" Hippolyta hated the whine she could hear rising in her voice, like a child wangling for something sweet.

"My heart is no harder than yours," Orithya answered, lifting the sword and once again starting the ritual passes. "But at least I'm realistic. Think, Hippolyta, think. Even if we could change her mind, we wouldn't be allowed in to talk with her. No one is. Especially not the women who agree with her."

"There are some who agree?"

"Of course," Orithya said, punctuating her statements with the sword. "Women who have borne sons themselves. Women with new infants. Women who are merchants and have spent time beyond our walls trading with other tribes. They understand at least, even if they do not agree entirely. But we warriors are upholding the law. No one gets in to see Otrere. No one."

"And whose ruling is that?" Hippolyta asked, though she already guessed.

"Valasca's."

"Of course."

Orithya had gone through the first set of passes—"The Guardian"—and was starting on the second—"The Death Watch." She turned a quarter, then a half, her back to Hippolyta.

"And once the child is dead," Hippolyta said, "what's to happen to Mother then?"

Orithya shrugged but didn't slow her movements. "I don't think there's any provision in the laws to execute a queen. I expect she'll be exiled into the world of men."

"No!" Hippolyta cried just as Orithya turned and faced her, bringing the sword straight down and stopping it abruptly at Hippolyta's shoulder. "How could she survive?"

"She could become one of their slaves," Orithya said. "Or one of their *wives*, which is just as bad." Her voice was as sharp as her sword, but there was a hint of pain in it nonetheless. She lowered the weapon so that it was tip down.

"What are you two *princesses* talking about?" intruded a voice.

Hippolyta turned. The speaker was Molpadia, her bow held loosely in her left hand. She was too far away to have heard any of their conversation.

"We're discussing tactics," Hippolyta answered sharply. "How to set an ambush for a she-cat."

Orithya could not repress a wry grin. "So you'd better be careful, Molpadia."

Molpadia reddened. "You'd both do well to be less haughty now that you're only common clay like the rest of us." Then she glared at Hippolyta, adding, "And *you'd* better plan how to slay your first man instead of mourning our ex-queen."

She turned and sauntered off.

Hippolyta made a face at her back.

"She's right, you know," Orithya said, sheathing her sword.

"She's a sow," Hippolyta answered.

"Perhaps, but she's a brave fighter nonetheless, and we're going to need her when Valasca marches against the Phrygians." Orithya rolled her shoulders and stretched her arms out.

"The Phrygians! I thought Mother made peace with them," Hippolyta said. She suddenly wondered if the baby's being a boy had given Valasca an excuse to do what she'd been planning all along. As war queen, Valasca always preferred fighting to peace.

Orithya's mouth thinned down, and for a moment she was silent. Then, as if repeating something she'd heard, she said stolidly, "We can never be at peace with the rulers of men."

It was to be the last word of their conversation, for Hippolyta's two keepers strode across the grass and gathered her up for the march back to the barracks.

CHAPTER FOUR

A VOICE IN THE NIGHT

On the eve of the half-moon Hippolyta could scarcely fall asleep. She'd worn out her body with chores, with sword practice. She'd even gone hunting with the guards, coming back with two hares and a partridge for the barracks' pots.

But now, exhausted, as she lay on her long cot trying to sleep, sleep would not come. Instead her mind turned again and again to her mother in prison.

All around her she could hear the easy breathing of the other girls. Hippolyta turned over onto her left side and forced herself *not* to think of her mother. But then her traitor mind left the prison and fled to the Temple of Artemis with its wooden statues and its stone altar. She'd often been there on the full of the moon when all the inhabitants of Themiscyra came together for the sacrifice.

A sheep.

A heifer.

A goat.

A hare.

These were the thanks given to the goddess from a grateful people: beasts without the capacity to speak or think or feel.

But never—at least not since Hippolyta could remember—had a human being been sacrificed there.

And certainly never, *ever* a baby.

Hippolyta's thoughts seemed to spin out of control, drenched in red, blood red. She turned onto her right side, then again onto her left. No place in the bed seemed free of those visions.

But at last sheer exhaustion began to drag her down to a restless sleep. It was then, as she slipped into a dream, that she heard a voice calling her name.

"Hippolyta," it said in her ear, "arise and come to me."

She sat up and looked around suspiciously. There was no one in the room but the sleeping girls.

The voice came again. "Hippolyta, say not a word. Come to me."

At first she thought the voice was simply part of her dream. But when she pinched her arm, right past the wrist, it hurt.

Quickly Hippolyta slipped into her leggings and

tunic and grabbed up her cloak. She jammed her cap on her head, then followed the voice out of the dormitory and into the street outside. The guards were soundly asleep.

The way was in shadow, partly lit by the half-moon. A small breeze puzzled along the street.

Suddenly she felt foolish outside by herself in the middle of the night. She turned to go back in.

"Hippolyta." Her name was called again, and this time a robed figure leaned out of the darkest shadows.

"Who's there?" Hippolyta cried. Then she saw by the way the figure leaned that it was Demonassa. The old priestess chuckled, like a girl enjoying a prank.

"How could you call me from so far away?" Hippolyta asked. "How could you be sure I was the one who heard and not one of the other girls? Or one of the guards?"

For a moment Demonassa looked affronted. "Am I not a priestess? Is there not magic in my very fingertips?"

Hippolyta sucked in a long breath. She'd always thought the magic of the old woman consisted mostly of drugged smoke and misdirection. "Then what do you want of me, priestess?"

Instantly Demonassa became serious. "Don't you want to see your mother?"

"Of course."

"Well, I've come to take you there."

"Ah." Hippolyta let the breath out again. "Do you think I'll be able to change her mind?"

Demonassa snorted. "You might as well try to turn the river away from the sea."

"Then you approve of what she's doing?"

The old woman smiled. "I approve of anything that galls Valasca."

Hippolyta was astonished and glad of the night so that her face would not give her away.

Demonassa knew anyway and laughed. "I have shocked you, daughter of Otrere. Well, I am old, and I am a priestess and am allowed my little jokes. But that is not the entire reason I support Otrere's decision. She is a good woman and a great queen. She did not make the decision to keep the child alive lightly. Besides, I have learned enough of the ways of the gods to know that their prophecies are not always to be trusted. They use prophecy to bully us poor mortals. They speak in riddles and not straight on. If they wanted us to be guided by truth, they would say clearly what they mean instead of wrapping their words in mist and smoke. And I can*not* believe that the gods would want the death of an infant as a price for their support."

She raised a finger. "But come. The night wears on, and we have but little time." The finger went to her lips, and then she turned and scuttled down the street, like a dung beetle over a midden heap.

Hippolyta followed after her silently, and soon they

came within sight of the square block of the prison. The old woman held up her hand, and Hippolyta stopped.

"How," whispered Hippolyta, "can we possibly get in without being seen?"

"Philippis watches your mother's cell tonight," Demonassa said carefully. "I saved her daughter from the fever last year, so she owes me this favor—and her silence. Besides, she agrees with what your mother is doing."

"Is she alone?"

"Her fellow guard had to retire with indigestion an hour ago," Demonassa said.

"How . . . fortunate," Hippolyta whispered.

"My fault, I'm afraid." The old woman had that childish glee in her voice again.

They went silently on, two shadows in a night of shadows, and when they came to the door, it was opened from inside. Philippis passed a long metal key to the priestess and then, pointedly, averted her eyes.

Demonassa led Hippolyta by the hand along the hall and to one cell, which she unlocked. Pulling the door slightly open, she gestured to Hippolyta. "Go in," she whispered.

Hippolyta slipped through the opening and entered the cell. The room was small and cramped, with a hard rush-covered floor. A small amount of moonlight filtered in through the grille in the wall, but it was barely enough to see by. Queen Otrere was sitting on a bench beneath the window.

The minute Hippolyta entered, Otrere rose to embrace her. Hippolyta was astonished at how thin her mother was. She could feel the small bones in Otrere's back. Yet when Hippolyta looked carefully, her mother seemed remarkably composed.

As if, Hippolyta thought, *stripping away the trappings of rank only revealed how much of a queen she truly is.*

"How have you all been, daughter?" Otrere asked at last.

"Well enough, Mother," Hippolyta answered. She did not mention Antiope's grief. No need to worry her mother more than necessary. "A proper bed and decent meals. But you—you're much too thin. We've heard stories that they're starving you, and—"

"Don't listen to gossip, child. I'm treated no worse than any other prisoner." Otrere smiled wryly. "And when Philippis is on duty, much better."

"But you aren't just *any other* prisoner, Mother. You're the queen!" Hippolyta's voice, though low, was full of anger.

"Not anymore," Otrere said. "But seeing what discord among the people my arrest has provoked, Valasca has asked that I give my blessing to the sacrifice. If I do that much, she promises I'll be restored to the throne."

"Then *do* it!" Hippolyta said. Her voice was louder

than she meant, and she immediately clamped her hand over her mouth.

"Never!" Otrere whispered hoarsely. "I will forbid this awful act as long as I have the breath to resist."

Hippolyta was silent for a moment, then said, "Mother, if you continue on this path, what will happen to all your good work? Even now Valasca is using your actions and your absence as an excuse to mount a campaign against the Phrygians."

Otrere leaned forward. "Do you know this for certain, daughter, or is it more gossip?"

"Orithya told me."

"Your sister is not in the councils of the Elders," said Otrere. "She can't know what they're planning. But if she's right . . ."

"If she's right," Hippolyta said quickly, "then you must take your throne back quickly. Give up the boy, Mother. What a small payment to save your people."

"Small? You call the murder of an infant a small payment? How dark a fate will fall upon us if I approve the murder of my own babe!" her mother replied.

"But he's only a male," Hippolyta said. "He should mean less to you than your own race. The laws say so. Surely other queens have given up their sons on the altar."

Queen Otrere smiled sadly. "No, Hippolyta, I am the first of the queens to give birth to two live sons."

"Then indeed the prophecy has come true . . . and the laws."

Otrere shook her head. "Oh, my dear daughter, our laws may determine how we must act, but they can't dictate how we feel. Would you sacrifice one of your sisters if the laws demanded it?"

"That's not the same."

"Isn't it?" her mother said quietly. "That baby is your brother."

"*Brother* . . ." Hippolyta screwed up her face. It was a rare word in the Amazon language, and it sounded strange to her.

"Yes, your brother, blood of your blood." Queen Otrere glanced out the grille at the moon, which was now low on the horizon. "Same mother, though different fathers. That's why I'm counting on *you* to save him, to bring him to his father."

"Me?" Hippolyta was horrified. Her hand went to her breast. "Why me?"

"Who else is there?" her mother said in a sensible voice. Hippolyta hated it when her mother was so sensible. "Antiope and Melanippe are much too young to undertake such a difficult journey alone. Orithya is too close to Valasca for me to trust her. It has to be you, my daughter."

It has to be me. Hippolyta knew that much was true. She didn't like knowing that.

"But there's only one day left," she objected. "The baby will be well guarded. I don't know how to ride with an infant. What if I get hurt? What if I'm discovered?

What if he gets sick along the way?" She ran out of breath and excuses at the same time. Then she added in a whispery wail, "He's only a *boy*!"

Otrere sat down on the bench as if standing had wearied her. She folded her hands. Mouth firm, back straight, she sat as though a thousand pairs of eyes were on her, not just one. Hippolyta had seen her mother sit like that many times when passing judgment on a dispute between two of her subjects.

"As I am no longer queen, I can't command you to do anything," Otrere said. "But I can still ask it—as your mother."

Hippolyta felt a chill run through her. "It will mean going up against Valasca and *all* of the others. And against the goddess's law." She waited, hoping to change her mother's mind.

"If all are wrong, and only you are right, still you must do that right thing," Otrere told her.

"But I don't know what the *right* thing is," Hippolyta wailed again. She knelt and put her head in her mother's lap.

Otrere stroked her daughter's hair, feeling its tough wiriness. "It's not right under any circumstances to murder an innocent infant."

"But the law—"

Her mother sighed. "That law was made many generations ago by superstitious women so afraid they might once again fall under the rule of men that they wandered ceaselessly upon the earth. They tried to outdo men in cruelty, as if that were the only way they could be strong. We have come far beyond those women, Hippolyta. We must honor them as our mothers, but we have outgrown their fears. Today we live in a community within walls. We hold commerce with our neighbors, whether they be women or men. And we have learned to temper justice with mercy. That is our strength now."

"But what about the gods, Mother? Won't they be angry if we break our part of the pact and keep the child alive?"

Otrere lifted her daughter up so that they looked into each other's eyes. "Sometimes we have to make the gods angry." She laughed briefly. "It's often the only way to get their attention."

Hippolyta's jaw dropped. *"Mother!"*

Otrere stood and took Hippolyta up with her. "The news you bring me about the Phrygians lets me know absolutely that you must go. I must stay here opposing Valasca for as long as I'm able. If she is rid of me, she'll plunge our sisters into years of empty, bloody warfare. She is a throwback, daughter, to the old ways, the old fears. We must go forward, not fall behind. I am certain I can make our sisters understand this."

Valasca's hawk face suddenly filled Hippolyta's mind. She sighed. "I'll do it."

"Of course you will," Otrere said. "You're my good, brave girl."

"Do you have a plan?" Now that Hippolyta had said the words, had given her promise, she was eager to get started.

Otrere nodded. "Demonassa will bring Podarces to you tomorrow night."

"Podarces?"

Otrere smiled. "That's the baby's name. Podarces—swift-footed."

"Baby" seemed good enough to me, thought Hippolyta. But she didn't say it aloud.

Otrere went on. "A trusted acolyte will carry an orphaned baby girl that Demonassa has been caring for to the ceremony in his place. Only when the child is actually on the altar and stripped of its clothing will the substitution be discovered. Since it will be a girl, no one will touch the child, and the acolyte will lay the blame on Demonassa, who can escape with the aid of her magic. That will buy you time to be on your way."

"Where am I to go, Mother?" Hippolyta had been wondering this all along, even before she'd said she would take the boy.

"To Troy."

Hippolyta started. Troy was a very long way away. Days and days and days. She knew no one who'd ever been there. "Why Troy?"

Otrere smiled wryly. "Because that's where you'll find Podarces' father. Laomedon, king of Troy."

"He's a king's son?" How many more surprises might Otrere unfold this night?

"He's a *queen's* son," Otrere answered. "And should Valasca learn where he is, even *she* will think twice before assaulting the high stone walls of that city."

Hippolyta tried to envision a high-walled stone city filled with men and failed.

"You'd best go now," Otrere said. "Another guard may appear at any moment."

Hippolyta walked to the cell door, then turned. "Mother . . ." Already she was thinking that her mother had the right of it. The powerful king of Troy would surely send them help in exchange for his son.

Otrere was looking down at her hands.

"Mother, I swear I'll return and restore you to your throne."

As if she somehow had known the conversation was at an end, Demonassa appeared and led Hippolyta out of the prison. Hippolyta threw one last regretful glance back at the rough gray building before following the old seeress into the darkened streets.

"Don't worry about Otrere," Demonassa advised. "She has made a hard choice and knows how to abide by it. Now you must abide by yours. Go swiftly to your bed before anyone notices you're gone. Tomorrow will seem a long enough day."

CHAPTER FIVE

THE SACRIFICE

A s Demonassa had warned, the day wore on slowly. The sun almost seemed to have stopped overhead, as if the gods had decided to forgo night.

Hippolyta was convinced that anyone who so much as glanced in her direction could read on her face the outline of the plan. *Any minute,* she thought, *Valasca's guards are going to arrest me.* Then a second traitorous thought filled her mind. Perhaps arrest would be preferable to fulfilling her vow to her mother.

But though the day went by with agonizing slowness, it did go on. Hippolyta wasn't able to eat either her morning or noon meals, and by evening she felt sick with worry.

The other girls in the barracks ignored her, putting on their ceremonial cloaks and chattering. Then they formed up for the march to the Hill of Artemis.

Hippolyta watched them from her pallet, one hand over her head. She'd planned to feign illness, but having missed all her meals, and with her stomach in a turmoil, she didn't have to feign much.

A tall, gangly, horse-toothed girl of sixteen summers turned back and said over her shoulder, "Aren't you coming with us, Hippolyta?"

Hippolyta merely groaned and turned over in her bed.

"You must, princess," said another, her voice a high whine. "You'll lose face otherwise."

"Valasca will be furious," a third added.

Hippolyta answered them with a groan and held her stomach, and they, thinking it her moon time, stopped bothering her in case they were late for the ceremony themselves. Giggling, their voices like water over stone, they left.

As soon as she was alone, Hippolyta pulled on her riding clothes: tunic, leggings, cloak, cap. She grabbed her ax and bow and quiver from under the foot of her pallet and went out the door.

No one was in the street. The entire community would be at the sacred hill. Still, she went cautiously, pausing at every corner to be sure she wasn't seen.

Hippolyta knew a spot below the wooden palisade

where she could jump and land quite safely on a stretch of soft, grassy ground. All the girls knew of it. The place was far enough from the front gates and the guards. Often they would sneak out in the night and make their way to the river, where they'd swim, naked, in the moonlight, away from the hard eyes of their mothers and older sisters. Hippolyta was just beginning to suspect that the women knew of the place too, that they'd gone there in their own youth.

But it would serve her purpose this night.

In one quick, economical movement, she leaped from the palisade, landed with bent knees, rolled headfirst down the little embankment, and leaped up, ax ready.

But there was no one watching.

So she headed north to meet Demonassa.

For a moment she slowed, turned, looked to her left. She could see the ring of bonfires surrounding the Temple of Artemis. They looked like a crown of flames. Drums were pounding; she could feel the beat in her bones. A pipe shrilled, then another. Lines of torches marked the processions as other Amazons from the far settlements of Satira, Amazonion, Comana, and Amasia came for the sacrifice.

The sacrifice!

All this for a tiny baby.

My . . . brother, she thought.

Just then a shadow detached itself from the trees, and for a moment Hippolyta raised her ax. Then she recognized Demonassa.

As the old seeress had promised, she held the baby in her arms. He was so heavily wrapped, against both the night air and his own cries, even his nose was scarcely visible.

"No one saw you come?" Demonassa asked, the baby held against her shoulder.

"No one. And you?"

The old woman grinned, showing the gaps in her yellowed teeth. "On the night of the half-moon I can move about seen or unseen, as I choose." She handed the child to Hippolyta.

Hippolyta's arms seemed to move on their own. Suddenly she had no control over her fingers. *Nerves,* she thought. Until this moment everything had seemed like a dream. But now, with the baby's weight a reminder, she was frightened.

"Has no one noticed the child gone yet? Has no one noticed you missing?"

Demonassa shook her head. "My acolyte is wrapped in a spare set of my robes. Even now she sits hunched over a girl baby as if it were little Podarces. I'll be back at the temple and ready to bear the supposed sacrifice to the hilltop before anyone guesses the deception."

"But—" Hippolyta could think of a dozen things that could go wrong.

"If anyone grows suspicious, the girl is to act bewitched. I'll not have her take the blame."

Hippolyta nodded. Bad enough that she and Demonassa might be caught.

The old woman grinned again. "By law, no one may approach the babe until he is laid on the altar. After that, I'm afraid, the game's up."

"*Game!*" The word sat uncomfortably on Hippolyta's mouth. "This is no game."

Demonassa tightened the cloak around her old shoulders as if she had need for more warmth.

Suddenly Hippolyta realized that the old priestess was not as invulnerable as she pretended. "What will happen to you then?"

Smiling with thin lips, Demonassa said, "Oh, none of them dare actually harm me. Too many of them owe me their lives. But I expect Valasca will see that my remaining years are spent in acute discomfort."

She means prison, Hippolyta thought. *At her age it is a sentence of death.* She looked down at the child, who was quietly sleeping in her arms. "You would risk so much for a boy?"

"I risk it for your mother's sake. I trust her instincts more than I trust the oracles," Demonassa said. "You should do the same."

Hippolyta nodded, but in her heart she was not convinced.

"Go then," the old woman added. "There's a horse tethered out of sight beyond those trees, near Demeter's shrine."

"My own horse?"

"No," Demonassa said. "We couldn't take that one for fear of discovery. It's one of your mother's."

Hippolyta nodded again.

"There are rations and water for you, a skinful of goat's milk for Podarces. Feed him when he cries." She touched Hippolyta's shoulder, turned her, and gave her a small shove forward. "Goddess keep you." Then she was gone, back into the shadows.

The horse was right where the priestess had said it would be. Hippolyta smiled. Not just one of her mother's horses, but her swift-footed little brown mare, the one called Rides the Wind.

Hippolyta put her ax and bow and quiver into the blanket packs. Then she untied the mare and started to mount. But with the baby in her arms, she was awkward, and the little horse was agitated.

"This is not a good start," she whispered.

A familiar mocking voice suddenly rang out from behind her. "I thought you might be up to something."

Hippolyta whirled around, instinctively pressing

the baby to her heart.

Molpadia stood, bow drawn, under the near trees. Her yellow hair looked almost white in the moonlight. "That's even better," she said. "Now I can kill both of you with a single shot."

CHAPTER SIX

FIGHT

For a moment Hippolyta was too stunned to reply. Then the malicious satisfaction on Molpadia's face, its shadowy smile, galled her into speech.

"I'm surprised to see you here. Shouldn't you be carrying Valasca's spear for her?" Hippolyta put as much scorn as she could muster into her reply.

Molpadia's face grew dark and angry. "When I didn't see you at the ceremony, I asked the girls where you were. 'Crying in her bed,' they said. I didn't believe that. Your pride would never have allowed you to show weakness unless there was a purpose behind it."

"Thank you for the compliment," Hippolyta said sarcastically. But she scanned the area as she spoke.

As she suspected, Molpadia was alone, wanting all the credit for capturing her. *One slim advantage.*

"No compliment intended."

Hippolyta thought, *I must play to her sense of history, of destiny. The longer we talk, the more effort it will cost her.* She knew that holding a bow steady was nothing anyone could do for very long, not even Molpadia.

"If you kill the baby," Hippolyta said slowly, "you'll prevent the proper sacrifice from being performed. The goddess's anger might very well fall on you then, not on me or my mother."

"That may be true," Molpadia mused. Already the strain of holding the bowstring taut was starting to show on her face. "Or it may be that you're trying to get out of this by talking."

"What if I surrendered myself to you?" Hippolyta said. "You could have both the credit for capturing me and saving the baby for the sacrifice."

"Why don't I believe you?" Molpadia sneered. A sudden involuntary tremor ran up her bow arm.

"Maybe because you're an untrusting sort?" Hippolyta said, taking a cautious step forward.

Molpadia's grin was now as tight as the bowstring.

Hippolyta saw the grimace, and immediately made her move. She stepped nimbly to the right, then fell suddenly into a crouch, hunched over the baby to shield it.

Sensing the movement, Molpadia released the arrow, but she had not anticipated the crouch. "Curse you!" she cried as the arrow flew over Hippolyta's head.

As soon as she felt the whisper of air over her, Hippolyta rolled the baby onto the grass well to the side, turned, and charged before Molpadia could reach for a second arrow. Her head struck Molpadia hard in the stomach, winding her and knocking the bow from her hand.

They tumbled onto the grass together, Hippolyta on top of Molpadia for a moment. The older girl managed to flip Hippolyta off. Then she leaped on top of Hippolyta, panting angrily.

"Goddess help me!" Hippolyta cried.

"Why should she . . . listen to you . . . who would have robbed her . . . of her just . . . sacrifice?" Molpadia said, but her breath was coming in short gasps. She reached for the knife in her boot, but Hippolyta grabbed her wrist and held it firmly. In return, Molpadia seized a handful of Hippolyta's long black hair and jerked her head back violently.

Hippolyta yelped. "Has it come to this? That we kill one another instead of our enemies?"

"You *are* my enemy," Molpadia cried. "And Valasca's."

"I'm only the enemy of those who are unjust," Hippolyta replied passionately.

"The just follow the laws," Molpadia told her.

"The just follow their hearts," Hippolyta answered, still holding Molpadia's wrist with her left hand.

"Ha! You haven't the spirit of a true warrior. Don't

hold me. Fight me! Fight—if you are to have the name of Amazon."

All the while they challenged each other, Hippolyta's other hand had been desperately trying to find her own knife in its sheath. Instead it found Molpadia's quiver of arrows, slid halfway down her side.

"Amazons are much more than brute fighters," Hippolyta whispered, desperate to keep the conversation going so as not to alert Molpadia to what she was doing.

"What else are we, coward?" Molpadia cried.

Snatching an arrow from the quiver, Hippolyta held it firmly. "Smart fighters!" she said, jabbing upward with her last bit of strength and striking Molpadia in the shoulder with the arrow point. Then she fell back, exhausted, onto the ground.

Molpadia screamed, staggered upward, pulled the arrow out, and flung it away. Shoulder bleeding freely, she turned and scrambled over to where the baby lay on the hillside. Crouching over him, she held up her knife.

"I sacrifice you to Artemis, as our laws and history demand," she cried.

At Molpadia's cry, Hippolyta sat up. She remembered her mother's voice saying, "Keep the child safe." But he was long footsteps away. How could she possibly reach the child in time?

In the moonlight Molpadia's knife blade glinted.

Then Hippolyta saw, to one side, a figure moving

swiftly from beneath the protection of the trees. "Goddess!" Hippolyta breathed in surprise, and Molpadia looked up from her bloody task.

Before she could see what it was Hippolyta had seen, the haft of a spear cracked across the back of her skull, and she dropped without a sound. The knife slipped from her fingers.

Orithya stood over her, spear in hand. "That should keep her quiet till daylight. She'll have an awful headache come dawn."

"Praise the goddess you got here in time," Hippolyta said.

"Oh, I've been here for a while, little sister, but you were doing just fine. I saw no need to intrude." She grinned.

Hippolyta went over and picked up the baby. He had slept through the entire thing. "Molpadia was really going to kill him."

"And you next, I suspect. I was really saving you, not him. Otherwise Mother would never have forgiven me."

Hippolyta held out the baby to Orithya, but the older girl took a step back as if afraid any contact with the boy child might carry a curse.

"You know," she said in a tight voice, "it would be best for all if he just *fell* into the river."

"I swore to Mother that I'd keep him safe," Hippolyta said.

"Then wherever you're going, go swiftly. And don't—" She held up her hand. "Don't tell me where. The less I know, the better. And now I'd better get back to the sacrifice." Her mouth twisted oddly. "Or whatever it will be now. Valasca is sure to miss Molpadia, her little yellow-haired pet. It would be bad for me if we're both found missing." She helped Hippolyta mount the mare.

"Thank you, sister. May the goddess bless you," Hippolyta said, looking at her sister's familiar face shining through the hard mask of soldiery.

"Here," Orithya said suddenly. "Take this." She slipped the serpent bracelet off her arm.

"But that's your Long Mission bracelet. I don't deserve one yet."

"You may need it on your journey," Orithya said. "For I guess that journey will be longer and more dangerous than any Mission a young Amazon gets to take."

"But what will you do if they ask you about it?"

Orithya grinned. "Oh, don't worry. I'll have a bracelet. It's Molpadia who'll have some explaining to do. Now go."

Hippolyta grabbed the rope reins and pulled the mare's head around till she was facing west. Then over her shoulder she called to her sister, "I don't know what would have become of me without—"

"Go!" Orithya said again. "We both have little time."

Hippolyta kicked the little mare in the ribs, but as it started off, she glanced back one last time—at her sister disappearing behind the palisade and at the little town beyond it—and wondered when she might ever see them again.

CHAPTER SEVEN

CAPTURE

H ippolyta had been trained in the arts of hunting and war. She'd been taught how to live on berries and nuts, on wild onions and nettles. She'd spent whole nights on forced marches with her instructors and had to endure their frequent blows.

But she was *not* prepared for the journey to Troy.

The problem wasn't the endless hours of riding. Or the heat of the noonday sun. Or the cold nights on the hard ground.

The problem wasn't the fording of swift rivers or leading the horse through rock-strewn mountain passes or battling the armies of insects that seemed to attack both day and night.

The problem was the baby.

She wouldn't call him by his name.

Oh, she had expected to rear a child of her own someday, taking a temporary husband from one of the neighboring tribes so that she might give more life to the Amazon race.

Someday.

But she hadn't expected to have to care for a baby so soon.

She hadn't known that a baby would cry so much.

It cried when it was tired.

It cried when its breechcloth needed changing.

It cried when it was hungry.

It cried when it wanted attention.

It cried when it wanted to cry.

When the goat's milk ran out, Hippolyta had to hunt down birds and rabbits and trade them at lonely farmsteads for fresh milk for the baby. What was left over after the trade was scarcely enough to feed herself.

Finally, after two weeks of riding, she saved a wild she-goat in the hills of Phrygia from a pack of menacing wolves. Since the animal seemed to live on thistles and ferns—and air—it made an easy companion. The milk it produced was enough to feed the child.

But not enough to keep him from crying.

I could cheerfully kill him myself, she thought as he once more sent up that thin, fierce wail that seemed to pierce her straight through to the bone.

She pulled the little mare to a halt, slowing the goat

as well, for it trailed behind them, pulled by a long rope. Groping for the skinful of milk the goat had produced just hours before, Hippolyta shoved the makeshift teat into the baby's mouth.

At least when he is suckling, he's quiet, she thought. And cradling both the baby and the bottle in her left arm, holding the reins in her right, she kicked the mare on.

Bleating, the goat followed after.

Never, Hippolyta thought, touching her sister's bracelet with her forefinger, *never has there been a Long Mission like this.* She didn't know whether to laugh or cry about it. In the end she did neither.

By the time they reached the plain of Mysia, a journey of four weeks more—with yet another two weeks at least till Troy—Hippolyta was feeding and changing the baby by reflex. When he was cranky, she found he could be soothed with the lullabies her mother used to sing to her little sisters. If he tired of those, she sang the rousing hero ballads instead. He seemed especially to like the one about the great warrior queen Andromache, who won so many famous victories.

He began to cry less and learned to smile. He played with her hair, entangling his little fist in her long, straight black locks. When he got too big to carry easily in one arm, she made a sling out of her cloak and tied him to her back. He seemed to enjoy riding that way and spent hours alternately napping and contentedly watching the roadside.

Hippolyta began to think that perhaps he was not so bad after all—for a boy.

But she never gave him his name.

One night, when the boy was nearly sixty days old and they were well into the Lydian lands, Hippolyta fell asleep exhausted before even finishing her evening meal.

The fire had burned low, and the baby was asleep in his little hammock, slung between two trees, where he would be safe from any wolves or other scavengers.

Hippolyta was dreaming deeply. In her dream she saw the Hill of Artemis on the outskirts of Themiscyra. Moving closer, she noticed that something lay, bound hand and foot, on the altar.

When she got closer still, she realized that the one on the altar was herself and that she was gagged as well as bound so that she couldn't cry out.

Suddenly she was no longer looking down but looking up, terrified, waiting for death.

Around the altar were hundreds of Amazons, including her own mother and sisters, crying for her blood. Orithya was calling the loudest.

At that moment the priestess Demonassa appeared, a large, jagged dagger clasped in her bony fingers.

"A sacrifice must be made," the old priestess intoned,

raising the dagger. As she leaned over, her withered features seemed to melt and change till what stared down was the fierce and beautiful face of the goddess Artemis. The moon crowned her head, and winking stars glinted like jewels in her wild dark hair.

"You must atone for lost Arimaspa," Artemis cried, her voice like a fierce north wind.

The Amazons answered her in a single voice: "Arimaspa."

Then the dagger sliced downward, and Hippolyta felt a searing pain in her side.

She woke, and the pain only increased as a second boot struck her in the ribs.

Groaning, she pulled away. Traces of the dream still held her in their grip: the sea of feverish faces, the savage beauty of the goddess, the dagger . . .

Then she was wholly awake, blinking blearily into the dawn. Her ribs hurt, and somewhere to one side her horse was whinnying unhappily.

There were voices all around her, deep, coarse, hoarse.

The voices of men.

She sat up.

A pair of strong hands grabbed her tunic and pulled her roughly to her feet. "Why, it's just a girl in man's garb!" a man exclaimed.

Hippolyta aimed a kick between his knees and connected. He let her go, screaming. Someone else grabbed her, this time from behind.

"Let go of me!" she cried.

At the sound of her voice the baby began to wail.

For a moment the men looked confused. There were—she saw quickly—six of them, including the man behind her. They were dressed in plain tunics and sandals. Each was equipped with a helmet and bronze sword, and each had a shield hanging under his arm. Behind them, well away from the copse of trees, she could see the outlines of horses.

She aimed a second kick, backward, but this man was too quick for her. He tightened his grip, saying, "Mind yourself, girl."

"She's a wild thing, isn't she?" joked a broad-shouldered man with a broken nose and bad teeth. "But maybe there's a pretty face under all that dirt." He moved closer to peer at her.

All that dirt! Hippolyta was furious at the insult. She'd bathed three days earlier, in a lovely mountain pool, taking the baby in with her. They'd floated around for almost an hour, and he had gurgled and giggled and splashed until his lips had turned blue.

She spat at the speaker. He smelled like a horse himself.

A tall, hawk-nosed man yanked the other away. "We're not here for your entertainment, Lyksos," he said.

Then, nodding at the man behind Hippolyta, he added, "Let her go, Phraxos."

"But, Dares, what if she runs?" came a voice behind her.

"She won't go far without the child," the hawk-nosed Dares said. He stood squarely in front of Hippolyta, regarding her curiously.

She stared back at him. He had coarse dark hair covering his cheeks and chin, and his eyes were as hard as a shield. She'd seen men before, of course. Traders and merchants were sometimes allowed to enter the Amazon settlements, and she'd encountered a few others on her journey at the farmhouses where she traded for milk. But never had she met a man who looked so powerful.

And never before had any man laid a hand on her.

She shivered, then willed herself to stand tall. *An Amazon does not tremble before men*, she reminded herself.

"Escaped slave girl, do you think?" asked Lyksos. "That brat fathered on her by her master?"

"The child is not mine," she said quickly, "and I am no slave." There was anger in her voice, not fear. But her anger was not directed at the men. She was furious with herself for being taken so easily. What sort of Amazon was she to be caught asleep by these big, clumsy creatures? How could she have failed to waken at the first sound of their horses' hooves?

Then she put her anger elsewhere. *It's the baby's fault,* she thought. He'd woken in the night, and she'd spent hours soothing him. No wonder when she'd finally fallen asleep, it was into troubled dreams.

The one called Dares walked over to where a chubby-faced man was holding the baby, carrying him as if he were a rabbit trussed for the spit. Taking the child, Dares held him up and stared into his little face. Then, surprisingly, he clucked with his tongue, and the baby, who'd been just about to start caterwauling again, opened his mouth and smiled.

"Check to see if it's a boy or a girl," Dares said, handing the baby back to the chubby man.

"It's a boy," Hippolyta said quickly. "His name is Podarces."

"Swift-footed." Dares laughed. "Unlike his . . . companion."

Hippolyta felt her cheeks redden.

"Where do you suppose she got these weapons?" Phraxos said, turning over her pallet and holding up the ax and the bow. "Stole them?"

"They're mine," Hippolyta said, willing her voice to remain even.

A fourth man, with a ruddy complexion and a ring in his ear, started to laugh. "*Your* weapons?"

"Give them to me, and you shall see how well I use them," Hippolyta said. "On you."

"Impudent—" He raised his hand to strike her.

Dares seized him by the wrist. "Nyctos, put your hand down. She's speaking the truth. Look at that ax, the double-headed blade. Look what she's wearing—the pleated cloak, the fur cap. Look at the serpentine armlet. That signifies she's already made her journey into womanhood. She's an Amazon."

Nyctos shook his head. "Why would an Amazon be here alone?"

"Good question," Dares said, turning to look at her quizzically.

"I answer to neither you nor any man," Hippolyta said, but at the same time she felt some bit of pride at being identified.

"Maybe she's a scout for an attacking army," Lyksos suggested.

"With a baby boy for company?" Dares laughed. "Use your head, man."

"I hear they murder baby boys," said Nyctos.

"That's not true," Hippolyta said hotly. "I'm saving him."

Fast as a striking adder, Dares said, "Saving him from what?"

She closed her lips tightly together. The truth would not serve her here.

All at once the baby squealed, and half the soldiers were distracted. Hippolyta dived at Phraxos, pushing him off-balance. Grabbing her ax, she did a quick forward roll on the ground and came up on the far side of the men, holding the ax in both hands.

"You fool, Phraxos," Dares said. He motioned to his men, who, without a word, widely flanked her on both sides till she was inside a large circle with the baby on the outside.

Hippolyta's mouth went dry as a sun-baked rock. She could feel the blood pounding at her temples. Molpadia had taunted her about slaying her first man. How Molpadia would laugh now.

"Give me the child," she heard her own voice say, as if it were coming from somewhere far away. "And let me be on my way."

"Amazon or not, girl, you're no match for six Trojan warriors. Put down your weapon before we have to hurt you," Dares said. He held out his left hand to her, but the right hand held his sword at the ready.

"Trojans!" Hippolyta exclaimed. "But that's where I'm headed. I'm going to Troy to see King Laomedon."

The men began to laugh, a sound like growing thunder, but Dares silenced them with a raised hand. "And why must you see the king?" he asked.

"I have a message for him from Otrere, queen of the Amazons," Hippolyta said. "I'm her daughter, Hippolyta, Amazon princess."

At that the laughter became a cloudburst, and the sound of it made the baby cry.

"Surrender your weapon," Dares said, "and I promise to speak to the king for you."

"What proof do I have that you'll do what you promise?" Hippolyta asked.

"Only my word as a Trojan." He smiled, holding out his hand once again.

"Only your word as a *man*," she said, her voice full of scorn.

"That will have to do," Dares answered.

Hippolyta thought quickly. "Swear by your gods."

"Captain," said Phraxos, "let's just take her."

Nyctos grunted his agreement.

Dares held up his hand. "I swear by my gods that I'll speak to the king for you. You'll be our guest in Troy. Now give me the ax."

Knowing that she had gotten as much out of the man as she could, Hippolyta said, "And I swear by Artemis that if you're false, I *will* kill you."

The men began their thunderous laughs again. But again Dares stopped them. "Done, young Amazon princess. The ax?"

She gave him the ax, handle first, and the bow. They let her keep the arrows, which they considered useless by themselves. She smiled to herself. They hadn't seen how she'd used one on Molpadia.

Dares handed back the baby, and Hippolyta fed him the last of the milk. They let her milk the goat, then set it free. The horrid creature caprioled over the nearest hill and was gone, not even looking back once.

As she tied little Podarces on her back once again, she thought: *Stupid goat. I saved you from the wolves, and you run right back to them.*

Then Nyctos boosted her up onto the little mare, but Dares held the reins so that she couldn't even think about escaping.

And so, led by the Trojans, Hippolyta rode out of the small rounded hills and down into the city itself.

CHAPTER EIGHT

ON TO TROY

roy.

She'd expected Troy to be much like Themiscyra, perhaps a little larger, but nothing like this. Even her mother's brief description of stone walls hadn't prepared her. The walls were built of huge stone blocks, each the height and length of a tall man.

How had the Trojans managed to move them? she wondered. *Surely only a giant or a Titan could have budged such a colossal weight.*

The city didn't consist of the wooden lodges and single-story buildings she was used to. Rather the stone dwellings and palaces of the Trojans rose twenty and thirty feet above the ground, overtopping even the mighty walls.

She gaped at the sight, and once more the men began to laugh at her.

Riding by her right side, Lyksos said unpleasantly, "I suppose you Amazons live in holes in the ground."

She snapped: "A real warrior would not need such high walls to hide behind." But her heart was not really in her reply.

"We have many enemies," Dares said evenly. "It is their number that decides the height of our walls."

Hippolyta continued to stare at the stones, measuring them with her eyes.

"Gaze well upon these walls, little princess, and think what sort of man must have built them," Dares said. "That man is our king. Laomedon. Do you still want me to keep my promise?"

Hippolyta took a moment before answering, then said, "I *must* see him."

They rode closer, and soon to the west of the walls they could see a blue sea sparkling in the noonday sun. Hippolyta put her hand up to shade her eyes and stared. Half a dozen ships were beached on the sand, their masts dismantled, their sails laid out to dry. As she watched, men busily loaded sacks and jars from the ships onto wagons. Overhead a single black-and-white tern flew by.

"The Aegean Sea, princess," Dares said. "Across those waves pirates sail, seeking plunder and slaves. Our walls keep *them* out as well."

Hippolyta shuddered. Amazons never entrusted themselves to the sea.

They fell behind the convoy of wagons and followed them through the main gate. Seven guards saluted Dares as they passed.

"Hail, Captain," one called. "Good hunting?"

Inside Troy the people were as strange as the houses. Hippolyta saw men and women the color of sand, of earth, of tree bark, of mustard flower. She heard the oddest accents as the merchants loudly traded in the street: silks from Colchis, spices from Egypt, elaborate pottery from Crete.

On her back the baby laughed and cooed, waving his little arm at the banners and bangles. She laughed with him. Even if she was more prisoner than guest, Troy was quite a sight.

Soon Hippolyta became aware that she was not the only one staring. She was drawing some curious looks herself. Sitting straighter in the saddle, she turned her head slightly to whisper back to the baby, "Be quiet. You're the child of an Amazon queen. You're the king's child." But it did not stop little Podarces from his cooing appreciation.

They passed by a marble temple, high and magnificent. Hippolyta looked for signs of which gods ruled here. Over the lintel was the face of a woman in a warrior's helmet. Hippolyta drew in a quick, audible breath.

Dares saw her staring. "Pallas Athena," he said. "Inside the temple is a statue of the goddess." He smiled. "As long as the statue remains, Troy can never fall."

"You place your safety in a woman's hands," Hippolyta said thoughtfully. *Then surely their king will give me what I want in exchange for his son. Weapons and warriors to free my mother.*

"Our king knows how to use the gods to his advantage," Dares said with surprising bitterness.

"No one *uses* the gods," Hippolyta replied.

Dares didn't answer, but his lips were like a dagger's slash across his face.

The royal palace now lay directly before them. Compared with it, the Amazon palace was indeed little more than a hole in the ground.

The palace rose up three full stories. Garlands of flowers decorated the windows; painted shields were affixed to the walls.

"To celebrate our victories," Lyksos pointed out, grinning and showing his bad teeth.

On one side of the courtyard Hippolyta saw a team of four enormous horses being unhitched from a golden chariot.

"The king has returned from his morning ride, I see," said Dares. "That'll put him in a good mood. Lucky for you, little princess."

Hippolyta unstrapped the baby from her back and

handed him down to Dares. Then she dismounted. Turning, she saw the captain staring deeply into the child's face. She saw that he'd figured out exactly why she was here.

Without a word, Dares handed the child back to her. Then he gave his shield and helmet to Nyctos, saying, "I'll see all of you for sword practice before the sun is half down."

Hippolyta stared into the baby's face, as Dares had done. Podarces looked exactly like Antiope at that age. In fact the baby looked like all of Hippolyta's sisters: coppery hair and brown eyes. *Only I am different,* Hippolyta thought, *being black-haired and blue-eyed.* She'd never wondered about that before.

When she glanced around for Dares, he was already halfway up the steps to the entrance to the palace. He beckoned Hippolyta to follow.

She caught up with him, and they passed a line of pillars painted with lifelike eagles and serpents. Then they went through a wide doorway into an entrance hall. It too was painted, only the subjects of these walls were hunting and war.

In the entrance hall stood many men. Courtiers, she supposed, for they looked at ease and were all dressed alike, in graceful tunics with pleated skirts and high-laced sandals. *Certainly not the garb of warriors.*

Dares acknowledged their greetings with a curt nod and led Hippolyta on into the main body of the palace.

They walked along a gallery lined with statues: men wrestling, throwing javelins, fighting with short swords. Hippolyta tried not to stare.

Suddenly a boy came skipping around the corner. He was about nine years old, with russet hair and bright amber eyes. Eating a pomegranate and humming to himself, he was so lost in his own thoughts he almost collided with Hippolyta. She jerked aside to avoid the collision and almost lost her hold on the baby.

"Curse you!" she cried.

The boy pulled up short, swallowed a mouthful of fruit, and glared at her from heavy-lidded eyes. Then he noticed Dares.

"You're back!" he cried.

Dares bowed, little more than a head bob really.

"Did you fight any battles?"

"No battles, Prince Tithonus," Dares replied. "I think the Lydians are keeping to their side of the border after the ambush we caught them in last week."

"Like you," Hippolyta said, still angry at the boy, "the Lydians need to watch where they're going."

The boy turned to her, and this time he stared without any disguise. "Are you a barbarian?"

"An Amazon, my prince," Dares said quickly.

The boy wrinkled his nose and announced loudly, "She's dirty. Someone should give her a bath."

"And someone should teach you manners," Hippolyta said.

Dares gave her a warning frown, but the boy wasn't at all put off.

"Do your men let you talk like that?" he asked. "I thought barbarians beat their women and kept them in cages."

"We have no men," Hippolyta answered, "and no need of them, either."

"You're very savage for a girl." He considered her carefully. "Better not talk to my father that way."

"I will if he talks to me the way you do," Hippolyta declared. The baby in her arms began to fuss, for the sound of argument frightened him.

"Calm yourself, girl," Dares advised. "For the baby's sake, if not your own."

Hippolyta shrugged him off and walked down the hall. Dares followed after her.

"How can you bow and scrape to that spoiled brat?" Hippolyta asked.

"He's a prince," said Dares. "You'd best remember that."

"Well, *I'm* a princess," she replied. "You'd best remember *that.*"

"She's going to get in trouble, isn't she?" Tithonus called, running after them. "I'd like to see that."

Dares turned. "Prince Tithonus, please return to your quarters." His voice was low and respectful, but there was no arguing with it. "Your father will want to see this girl alone."

The boy raised his eyebrows. "Will he? I wouldn't. She smells."

"I *don't* smell," Hippolyta protested.

"She smells no more than any of us who've been out for days sleeping rough," Dares said, keeping himself between the two. "And less than most." He gave the boy a gentle pat on the shoulder to speed him on his way.

The prince kept glancing back as he walked away, but Dares let out a sigh of relief when the boy was finally out of sight.

Around the next corner was a pair of great doors guarded by two men carrying long and cruel-looking spears. They glowered at Hippolyta but gave way at Dares' command, turning to push open the heavy wooden doors.

This room was even more elegant than the rest. The ceiling seemed supported by the slenderest of carved pillars. A series of mosaic tiles, arranged in patterns, made up the floor.

In the center of the room was a pool of bright blue water. There two pretty young women in delicate silken robes were dabbling their feet.

On the far side of the pool a man as golden and maned as a lion reclined on a couch. He looked up languidly, like a great beast roused from sleep, his gaze settling on Hippolyta.

"Prisoner of war, Dares?" He sounded both self-assured and amused.

"No, my king," Dares answered, keeping his eyes firmly lowered.

The king looked searchingly at Hippolyta and the baby. Then he said, "People usually bow when they come before me." He said it softly, but even to Hippolyta it sounded like a threat.

"I am a princess of the Amazons. I bow before no man," she replied.

The king's head went back, and he roared with laughter. When he laughed, the rough planes of his face resolved into something resembling beauty.

Then he stopped laughing as suddenly as he'd begun and looked at Hippolyta again, his eyes narrowing. "I know what you are, little Amazon. I have seen many of your sisters. Even loved a few. What I don't know is why you've brought your little bundle here."

He stood and walked over to Hippolyta. He was tall and wide-shouldered. His golden beard poured down his chest like a glittering wave. His long white robe was trimmed in purple and cinched in by a silver belt studded with red and green stones.

In spite of herself, Hippolyta was impressed. *Surely Zeus himself looks no more kingly.*

"She's here because of the baby," Dares said.

The king leaned over and looked at the child, who reached out for his beard. "Why should this child concern me?"

"I must speak privately with you, King of Troy,"

Hippolyta said. "My mother, Otrere, commands it of me."

At her mother's name, King Laomedon looked up, for a moment startled. Then he snapped his fingers to summon one of the girls.

"Take the child, Artemesia. Treat it well till I ask for it again," he commanded.

"It's a boy," Hippolyta said, handing the baby to the girl. "His name is Podarces." *Strange,* she thought, *how reluctant I am to give up this little burden now.*

"All of you but this little barbarian leave me," commanded Laomedon.

"Your Majesty, are you certain—" Dares began.

Hippolyta wondered whether he wanted to stay for her protection—or the king's. She was about to say she could handle herself when Laomedon interrupted.

"Check the defenses on the north wall, Dares." He waved his hand. "I need no help from you here."

Dares bowed low and, with a final warning glance at Hippolyta, left the chamber.

CHAPTER NINE

KING LAOMEDON

he king walked over to a table and poured himself a cup of wine. He did it with deliberate slowness, like a great beast deciding its next move.

When at last he looked up, he asked, "What is your name, daughter of Otrere?"

"Hippolyta," she answered. "Princess of the Amazons."

"But not the oldest of Otrere's brats," he said.

"Second oldest," she admitted.

He didn't say anything for a long moment but drained the cup of wine halfway. Hippolyta felt every bit of the time stretching out, like a leash around her neck.

"Otrere," Laomedon mused. "Lovely copper hair. Amber eyes. Nice smile. We spent some time together. Twice." He grinned, and the wine glistened on his lips.

Hippolyta hated the way he spoke of her mother, as if she were a broodmare he'd owned.

"We last met some months ago, on the Phrygian border by Aphrodite's grotto." The smile grew broader as he remembered. "I asked her to stay longer, for she matches me in spirit. I like that. But she would not. You Amazons are a restless lot." Now the smile was incandescent, like a candle before it burns down a house. "Take her my warmest regards when you go."

"She needs more than your"—Hippolyta spit out the next two words as if they were some filth in her mouth—"warmest regards." Drawing in a deep breath, she said, "She needs more because of that child of yours."

"The child you brought?"

He's toying with me, Hippolyta thought. *He knows very well the child is his.* But she couldn't think why he should be doing so.

"Yes," she said, "your son. Do you deny that he is yours, King Laomedon?"

He shrugged, finished the wine, and set the cup back on the table. "I saw a resemblance to her. Not to me. Still, she has no reason to lie about such a thing. So, you've brought him to his father's house, as is your custom. Very well, princess, you've done your duty. If you go to the kitchens, they will feed you before you leave."

He reached across the table to a bowl of grapes and plucked several, ready to pop them into his mouth.

Hippolyta walked over and almost put her hand on his arm, before thinking better of it. "My mother needs your help," she pressed. "The mother of your son, Podarces, needs your help."

He paused, a grape halfway to his lips. "*My* help? Amazons never ask for help from men. They just use them to beget children and leave." There was an undertone of anger in his voice, as if some anger with Otrere's refusal to stay with him lingered.

"Because Mother wouldn't sacrifice the boy on Artemis' altar but sent him here instead, she's been cast in prison," Hippolyta told him.

This time the king looked at her with great interest. "But when she sent me Tithonus, there was no such trouble," he said.

Tithonus! That little . . . brat? The other brother? Hippolyta could not believe it. But she had to answer quickly and not show her surprise.

"It's against our laws for a queen to bear more than one live son," Hippolyta said, her voice barely a whisper. She would not tell him why.

A mocking smile lit Laomedon's handsome face and changed it horribly. "Now we come to it! You Amazons thrive on superstitions, like crows feeding on dead flesh. Ha!"

Why, he's just as brutish and selfish as any man, only

with a prettier face. Oh, Mother, how could you have let that face seduce you? Hippolyta thought. But then she realized she was being unfair. Her mother had sought out a king to her queen, power to her power, beauty to her beauty. Her only interest had been to bring forth a strong, handsome child. She had not expected a boy.

But Laomedon was still Hippolyta's only hope. She would have to put aside her disgust for him and beg for her mother's life. "Queen Otrere has been stripped of her throne and will be tried for sacrilege."

He popped a grape in his mouth. For a moment he savored the grape. "It is of no interest to me." He glanced down, savoring the look of astonishment on her face. "And what would you have me do, little princess? Lead an army into Amazon country and set Otrere back on her throne? Leave my own city unguarded, my people unprotected, to march my troops through our enemies and into a barbaric country to settle a quarrel between savage women? Do you think I'm mad?"

"My mother has given you a child," Hippolyta cried. "No, she has given you two children."

"So have many women. I will not go to war for them."

"So she means *nothing* to you?"

Raising an eyebrow, he said with slow deliberateness, "My horse means something to me. When he dies, I will get another. I value my sword, my shield, my guard."

Hippolyta couldn't contain her anger any longer. The man had mocked her, her mother, her people. She lashed out an arm and knocked the bowl of fruit from the table. Grapes flew in all directions.

"You're no king!" Hippolyta raged. "The lowest beggar in the streets has more honor than you."

"Guards!" he thundered. But even before the doors could be flung open, he grabbed her by the hair and threw her to the floor. "*I* am the king, and I will decide what is honorable here in Troy."

She looked up, more surprised than hurt. "May the gods curse you, King Laomedon."

His face darkened. "They already have."

Just then the guards burst in.

Laomedon ran a hand down his tunic, smoothing it. "Take her to the cells."

The guards seized Hippolyta by the arms and yanked her to her feet. She struggled against them, but they were too strong.

"You needn't be gentle," the king said as the men bundled her out of the door. "She's an Amazon, which means she has no tender female sensibilities to injure."

They hauled her out of a back entrance and across a bare yard where soldiers were practicing with their spears. She tried to kick at the men who held her, but they were used to such tactics.

One of the spear handlers yelled out, "Leave her with us for an hour, Caracus, we'll show her how to behave."

But the guards didn't reply, merely dragged her to a large stone building standing on the other side of the courtyard. There they hauled her through a thick wooden gate and on inside.

A stiff-legged jailer led them past a long row of locked cells from which hooting and cursing voices called out.

"Let her go!"

"Bring her here!"

"May your wounds never heal, jailer!"

"The gods look down on your injustice, Laomedon!"

They stopped in front of a heavy wooden door, which the jailer opened with a large bronze key. Then the two soldiers threw her inside.

Stumbling forward, she remembered at the very last minute to tuck in her head and roll. She fetched up against the far wall, humiliated but unhurt. She heard the soldiers laugh uproariously as they slammed the door shut.

Struggling to her feet, Hippolyta felt a twinge in her shoulder, where it had struck the wall. The roots of her hair stung where Laomedon had grabbed her. She must have twisted her ankle slightly when she tumbled into the cell. But what hurt most was her pride.

She limped over to the cell door, glad no one could see her, and looked out of the small grille. She could see neither soldiers nor jailers.

Which doesn't mean there's no one there, she

reminded herself. *Only that I cannot see farther.*

Wrenching herself away from the grille and the light, she began to pace the confines of the cell. It was a much bigger place than the one her mother lay in, back in Themiscyra. But that cell at least had been clean. This one was disgusting. The walls were dank, the floor scattered with a thin layer of dirty straw.

Hippolyta tested the door with its small barred window.

Thick, sturdy, unmovable.

She felt along every inch of the walls.

Even thicker, sturdier.

She sat down on the floor to think. But every thought led back to one: *I have no friends here, no allies. I am at the mercy of a heartless king.*

In the evening—she knew the time only because the jailer told her so—she was given a bowl of thin, cold gruel. An armed guard stood by her as she ate, to prevent any trouble.

"Eat up," sniggered the jailer. "We want meat on you for tomorrow."

She dashed the empty bowl at him, but it missed, and the guard struck her in the chest with the butt of his spear. She fell backward, managing to miss hitting her head on the wall. But she lay there, pretending to be knocked out. That way she could avoid more of a beating, and quite possibly she might hear something to her advantage.

The sniggering jailer said, "Spirited all right."

The guard grunted. "Not that it'll do her any good. She's scarcely a bite as it is."

They left, locking the door behind them, and darkness seeped into the cell.

Scarcely a bite! What did they mean? She'd heard of kingdoms where prisoners were thrown to wild animals. Or maybe Laomedon was that vilest of creatures, one that devoured his own kind.

She shivered and started to whimper. Then she stopped herself. "Amazons do *not* cry," she whispered.

But she was cold, hurt, lonely, scared, and a long way from home.

She didn't cry. But in her sleep, something wet ran down her face from her eyes. She wiped it away without ever waking.

CHAPTER TEN

A BROTHERLY VISIT

he woke from a deep sleep when someone tapped on her door. Flinching back, she rubbed sleep from her eyes. Then curiosity overcame her, and she went to the door.

Standing there was the horrid little prince, Tithonus. "Shh," he said.

She thought: *If I can get him in here, I could take him hostage. Then they'd have to release me and—*

"Shh," he said again, finger to his lips. "Don't wake the others."

Her plans for escape gave way to curiosity. "How did you get in?"

He looked puzzled at her question. "Why, I told the

jailer to let me in. I'm the prince, after all. I said I'd have him thrown in the sea if he didn't do as I commanded."

"Yes, that's exactly what your father would have said," Hippolyta noted sourly. Suddenly she couldn't bear the sight of him. He was just a stupid, boastful, overindulged little boy playing a prank. "Go away," she said sullenly, moving back from the door.

"What?" He seemed genuinely shocked.

"I said—" and she spoke slowly over her shoulder as if talking to a tiny child—"go . . . a . . . way."

There was a pause. Then Tithonus said, "You're really not very nice, are you?"

Hippolyta sighed. "No, I'm not. I'm not nice. I'm a barbarian—remember? And I need my sleep. So go away." She found the small pile of dirty straw that served as her bed and sat down.

"No. I don't want to. I want to ask you a question," the boy said. "About my mother." He no longer sounded so pleased with himself. In fact he sounded as if he were on the edge of pleading. "The queen of the Amazons."

Hippolyta looked up sharply. She could not see his face at the grille. He was too short for that. "How do you know—"

"Father told me. Tonight. I'd always wondered . . ." His voice was now a small boy's, light, uncertain.

Sighing, Hippolyta stood and went back to the door and stared through the grille. For a long moment she looked down at him. In the torchlight, his hair was darker, almost brown. There was a shadowy smudge under one eye.

"Her name is Queen Otrere," she said at last. "She's my mother too."

"Then," he said slowly, "we're family."

She shook her head. "No, we're not. I left my family back in Themiscyra. My mother and sisters. Your family is here."

"But we share—"

"Blood. We share blood. That's all. Now go away. Or get me out of here." There, she'd said it. Without whining or pleading.

"I brought you a pastry," he said. His skinny arm reached up and into the grille. There was a dark circular something in his hand.

Hippolyta hesitated to take anything from a son of Laomedon, but it was too tempting. She snatched the honeyed pastry from his fingers before he had a chance of pulling it away.

"You must be very hungry, sister," he said.

"I've been hungrier," she replied. "And don't call me *sister*!" She ran a finger across her lips to wipe up the rest of the honey, then sucked greedily on the finger like baby Podarces on the wineskin teat.

"Don't bother to thank me," he said, now sullen. The shadows only deepened the pout on his face.

"You came here to ask a favor of me, boy. I've asked you for nothing." Hippolyta drew back a bit from the grille. *Except*, she thought, *to get me out of here or go away. Neither of which he's done.*

"You should thank people when they're kind to you."

She moved forward again and leaned right up against the bars. "Kind would be a soft bed and a clean bath. Kind would be somewhere away from here. I'll thank you when you set me free."

He backed away a step, then moved forward again. "Our father won't allow it."

She shivered. "*Your* father, not mine." But she wondered.

Tithonus was silent.

"Your father doesn't care if our mother lives or dies," Hippolyta said. "I asked him to help her, and he laughed. Then he threw me in here."

"He's—it's . . . hard work being king. He doesn't have time for everybody." Tithonus' face got a pinched, closed look.

Hippolyta laughed. "Ha! Not even time for his son's mother." Then she realized that he had sounded sad, almost apologetic. Suddenly she understood. In a quieter voice she added, "So he's got no time for you, either, eh?"

"That's not true!" Even in the flickering torchlight she could see him flush. His chest was heaving. "Dares— Dares says that things are hard. We're surrounded by enemies and—" He shut his lips together as if he'd admitted too much. "I just wanted to know about *her*. About Queen Otrere."

"What do you want to know?"

The boy leaned forward, whispered eagerly, "What does she look like?"

Hippolyta backed away for a moment, thinking. The father was out of her reach, but not the son. She smiled grimly and went back to the grille. "She's ten feet tall with big purple eyes. She has snakes for hair, and she eats little boys for breakfast!"

Tithonus' lower lip quivered, and he disappeared into the blackness. She could hear him trying to stifle his sobs.

Serves him right, Hippolyta thought. But she felt bad. He'd been such an easy target. And he *had* brought her a pastry.

She called out, "Pssst. Prince. I'm sorry for saying that. Come back tomorrow and bring me two pastries, and I promise I'll tell you what you want to know."

He came back into the light, looking a bit whey-faced. "Tomorrow? But tomorrow will be too late."

She felt a stone in her stomach. "Too late for what?"

"Too late for you," he whispered.

"What do you mean?" The stone in her stomach got heavier.

But he was gone, running off down the corridor as though in fear of his life.

Hippolyta went back to the little pile of straw and sank down onto it. Any impulse to sleep was now gone. She was suddenly and awfully wide awake.

What has Laomedon planned for me? she wondered, remembering the guard's words: "Scarcely a bite." Remembering the king saying that he was cursed. Remembering that she had lashed out at him. At a king. In his own country.

I guess I'm going to find out, she thought miserably. *And soon.*

CHAPTER ELEVEN

CONDEMNED

he hadn't meant to fall asleep again. She thought she was wide awake. But suddenly the shouts and screams of the other prisoners woke her.

The door to her cell opened slowly, and in came the stiff-legged jailer with a sour look on his face. Behind him a guard stood at the door watching while the jailer thrust a dry crust of bread and a cup of brackish water at Hippolyta.

"Why they even bother . . ." he began.

She grabbed the bread and water and downed them. "Fattening me up, I suppose," she said, thinking to get information from him.

He looked startled. "You know?"

She nodded, hoping he would continue.

"Poor girl," he said solemnly, and took the cup from her.

"Aye," said the guard, "a waste of a good-looking woman, if you ask me."

"If you ask me," the jailer said as he went through the door, "she's too young by half for what you're thinking."

"Too young for what the king's thinking, too," the guard replied, shutting the door and locking it.

Well, Hippolyta thought, *that was a lot of help.*

She now knew enough to be thoroughly frightened without knowing anything at all. *But if I must die, I'll die bravely. Like an Amazon.* With that resolve, she sat down again on the dirty straw to calm herself.

She tried to remember the death chant she'd been taught. The one Queen Andromache had composed before the battle in which she'd been slain.

> *"I come to you, Artemis, with a clean heart,*
> *I come, Ares, ax in my strong right hand.*
> *My bow is strung. It sings my death song.*
> *My arrows are ready for flight.*
> *I come over the mountains, capped with snow,*
> *Past the eagles in their aeries,*
> *Past the far streamers of clouds. . . ."*

But in fact, she was bowless and axless and without her quiver of arrows. What good was singing a warrior's death song when it was clear that she was going to die badly, eaten by some awful . . . thing? And without being given the chance to fight.

Besides, she had failed her mother, failed her people.

Ashamed, Hippolyta began to weep.

By midmorning, when Laomedon's soldiers came for her, Hippolyta had recovered herself. She had even scrubbed her face clean of tears—or at least as clean as she could with the back of her hand—and she was standing up, waiting for the guards.

She'd heard them coming. A *Phrygian* could have heard them coming! They marched noisily along the corridor, the other prisoners taunting them, and that had given her time to stand tall, shoulders straight, head high. Like an Amazon.

The jailer opened the door, and the soldiers marched in. There were eight of them.

Eight men to one Amazon, she thought. *Just about right.* They pushed her out of the cell, binding her wrists before her. She walked—no, she strode—ahead of them.

Let them see how an Amazon dies, she thought.

But instead of being taken immediately to a place of execution, she was brought into a courtyard. There a gallery of courtiers had been assembled. All men, she noted with growing anger.

At all the exits bronze-armored soldiers stood guard.

Surely Laomedon doesn't think I'm that dangerous! she thought with a bitter smile.

Horses had been led from the stables and were even now being hitched to four chariots. Hippolyta recognized hawk-nosed Dares, who was supervising the operation. He glanced over, nodded, and for a moment looked as if he wanted to say something. But then he turned his back and finished the work he was set to do.

Just then there was a stir among the assembled courtiers, a kind of hushed buzz like a hive of honeybees, and the king came through a great door. He was accompanied by an armed escort. Dressed in a luxurious purple robe, he wore a golden crown and enough jewelry around his neck to hang himself. He was handsome and arrogant, every inch the king. Climbing five steps to a wooden throne, he surveyed the scene with languid ease.

The courtiers all clapped, and one man sang out, "The king! The king!"

Hippolyta's guards dragged her forward until she was directly in front of the throne. The king was seated high enough that she had to look up at an uncomfortable angle in order to look him in the face. She did it despite the discomfort. She didn't want to give him the pleasure of seeing her bow her head.

A stout, gray-bearded man came from the gallery and cleared his throat.

"Announce the charges, Argeas," Laomedon commanded.

Argeas cleared his throat again, before saying, "The barbarian girl Hippolyta—"

Hippolyta interrupted. "I'm no barbarian. I'm an Amazon, daughter of Otrere, queen of Themiscyra."

The gray beard began again. "The Amazon girl Hippolyta is accused of laying hands upon the royal person, threatening the king, and thereby assaulting the safety of Troy."

"I will show you *my* bruises, old man," Hippolyta interrupted, "and then you can decide who has assaulted whom."

"Silence, girl," Argeas said. "You don't have leave to speak. The first time you interrupted I said nothing, for you do not know our customs. The second time I instruct you. Let there be no third time, or woe befall you."

Hippolyta snorted. "More woe than being eaten?"

Old Argeas looked startled and turned to his king. "There can't be a sentence before the trial, Your Majesty."

Laomedon leaned forward. "*I* was the one assaulted, and *I* am the sole witness, and *I* am the judge. The girl is guilty. Trial over. Now we'll sentence her. Does that satisfy you, Argeas?"

The old man looked down. "Death is the sole penalty prescribed for such a crime, Sire."

"Then take her away and see that the sentence is carried out," Laomedon said. "Now let's move on to more important business."

The soldiers took Hippolyta by the arms and led her

toward the chariots. She twisted around and shouted back at Laomedon. "False king," she cried. "May the gods all curse you. May the Amazons come and lay waste to your city. May your walls be thrown down and the stones used to plug up your harbor. May Ares and Artemis loose the hounds of Hades to gnaw on your bones."

"Shut her up," Laomedon commanded, and one of the soldiers clapped a broad hand over her mouth.

But Dares stepped forward. "My lord," he said, "no one in Troy questions your justice. But mightn't we show this girl mercy? She's little more than a child. A barbarian. She hasn't been taught how to behave in a civilized society."

"Then this will serve as a sharp lesson to her. And for any little barbarian girls who come after," Laomedon said. "And I must wonder, my *loyal* Dares, why you should take her part." He dismissed Dares with a wave of his hand.

Dares sighed and mounted the front chariot. Hippolyta was pushed up beside him, and her wrists were tethered to the chariot rail. Then Dares flicked the reins, and the horses began to pull. The chariot bounced and jounced along the rutted road, and it was all Hippolyta could do to stay on her feet.

Behind them, in the other three chariots, an escort of soldiers followed.

Hippolyta looked back.

At the soldiers.

At the high walls like stone scabs over suppurating wounds.

At Troy.

CHAPTER TWELVE

MONSTER FROM THE SEA

"Where are we going?" Hippolyta asked in a hoarse whisper, not trusting her voice otherwise. Her wrists were already beginning to ache and her fingers to go numb.

Dares didn't turn to look at her. Instead he stared ahead at the road. At last he spoke, his voice held tight as if he were afraid it might break. "To a headland a few miles north of the city."

"A headland?" She tried to think. Would they try to drown her? She could swim a bit. A little bit. But she'd only paddled in slow rivers amid quiet pools, never in the sea. She pulled against the restraints, but they held fast.

"I warned you, girl," Dares said, still staring straight ahead. "I warned you to be careful in the presence of the king."

"May he be torn apart by harpies!" Hippolyta cried.

Dares ignored her outburst. "I told you to read the character of the king by the height of his walls, but you didn't listen. We Trojans have paid dearly for those walls." He snapped the reins against the horses' backs, and the horses leaped forward. "You will pay dearer yet."

"What have the walls of Troy—" Hippolyta started to say, but her teeth clattered together because of the rough ride, and she couldn't continue.

Used to the chariot's bounce, Dares had no trouble speaking. "Many years ago the gods Apollo and Poseidon plotted against their father, great Zeus. When he found them out, Zeus exiled them to earth to serve King Laomedon for a year as laborers. Laomedon had them haul those great stones all one hot summer. When their task was done, they demanded payment, but Laomedon refused."

"That doesn't surprise me," Hippolyta said, leaning forward to ease the ache in her wrists.

Dares' face was grim, his lips like a scar. "The gods were not amused, child. Poseidon sent a huge sea monster to terrorize our land. It is still here, regularly smashing the outlying farms and devouring anyone who dares live outside the walls of Troy."

"So, I suppose, then, that I am to be a tribute to that

monster," Hippolyta said, her voice strangely calm. Now that she knew, she was no longer afraid.

Dares nodded, unsmiling. "The headland is where the monster comes ashore to feed," he said. "As long as it eats its fill there, it goes no farther inland. Anyone the king condemns is chained out there on the rocks."

"Can you leave me my battle-ax, my bow?" Hippolyta said. "Chain me if you must, but let me die fighting. Please, Dares."

He shook his head. "I cannot, child. I cannot. But your death will be swift. That I *can* promise you." Never looking her way, he slashed the reins once again against the horses' backs, as if the sooner they got there, the sooner she would be at peace.

Suddenly she remembered her dream: the sacrificial altar, the jagged knife slicing down. "Oh, Artemis, dread goddess," she cried out loud, "I rescued a child from your altar. Now it seems I am to be the one sacrificed in his stead."

They entered a stretch of country that was barren and abandoned. As the chariot rumbled over the ill-kept road, Hippolyta noticed the smashed ruins of buildings, ripped-up trees, the skeletons of sheep and cattle.

"No one ventures here anymore," Dares told her.

"Unless they're bringing sacrifices," she added.

He nodded.

The headland ended in a rugged outcropping of rock

from which a gray ledge jutted out over a small shingle and the sea.

Obeying Dares' reluctant command, the soldiers climbed out of their chariots and dragged Hippolyta out onto the ledge. There they stood her between two gnarled pillars of stone and lashed one of her wrists to each pillar. The rocky slope dropped away to where waves rasped over a narrow stretch of shingle, making it difficult to stand upright.

Once the soldiers had secured Hippolyta, Dares sent them away. He drew his sword and spoke softly. "If you'd like, child, I can end this quickly for you now. The king will never know. It's all the gift I can give you."

Hippolyta stared for a moment at the blade. That would not be a hero's death, not the death of an Amazon princess. And though only Dares and she would know, she could not bring herself to ask for the quick, easy sword thrust. She shook her head.

Dares sheathed his sword and glanced at the sea. "The monster won't appear till dusk. The wait will not be easy. Pray to your gods, child." For a half breath it seemed as if he wanted to say more, but instead he shook his head and abruptly left.

Hippolyta tugged at her bonds, but her hands were securely fastened and in such a way that she had no strength with which to pull. After a furious struggle, trying to saw the leather thongs against the stone, she realized that she couldn't free herself that way.

She looked down at the lapping waters. How peaceful the sea seemed. One part of her refused to believe the story of the monster coming out of that undisturbed water.

"Perhaps," she whispered to herself, "perhaps Laomedon just wants to frighten me into submission." She gave a little barking laugh. "That would be just like him."

But the ruined buildings, the bones of cattle and sheep, had told a different story. Deep inside she knew that this was no stupid game.

The hours dragged by. When Hippolyta tried to relax against her bonds, the pressure on her shoulders was agonizing. She had to keep her legs straight, even though they ached with stiffness.

"Artemis," she said at last, "if you won't free me, at least give me the courage to face the end like an Amazon."

There was no answer to that prayer.

Hippolyta licked her dry lips and studied the waves, waiting for some sign of movement. That was when the sun plunged down in front of her, casting the sea in crimson, like a great puddle of blood.

Perhaps, she thought, *I will grow tired enough to fall into a swoon.* Which was about as much mercy as she could hope to get from the gods. It was certainly more than Laomedon would have granted her.

Laomedon. Suddenly she knew how to pray.

"Poseidon, Apollo," she cried aloud, "you whom Laomedon has offended, grant me a means of escape, and I will see that he suffers for what he's done."

Barely finishing her desperate prayer, she heard a scuffling sound to her left, and she tried to turn to face the noise. *Better to see my death than be surprised by it,* she thought. But she couldn't twist her head around enough.

Something was coming down the path, scrabbling and sliding without fear of being heard.

But the monster was to come from the sea!

Is there more than one serpent? she thought. *More than one killer?*

"Who's there?" she cried out. "Don't come closer. I'm armed. I'll hurt you."

But the scrabbling continued for a long minute, and then suddenly a small figure stood in front of her, smiling wanly.

"Tithonus!" Hippolyta cried. "What are you doing here?"

The prince's fine clothes were covered with dust, and his face was gray with fatigue. It looked as if he'd come all the way from Troy on foot.

"I had to see you," he said. "So I sneaked out of the palace. I had to walk. I—I don't know how to hitch up a chariot."

"See me—for what?" Hippolyta licked her dry lips again. "To mock me?"

"No, no, not to mock you." His face screwed up. "You look awful."

"I've been better."

"Do you want something to drink?" he asked, offering the goatskin that hung from the leather strap across his shoulder. He pulled the stopper and held it toward her.

Hippolyta pulled at the thong fastening her right hand. "I can't take it by myself."

He moved closer and raised the skin to her lips, clumsily pouring some water into her mouth. It trickled down her chin and neck.

"Trying to drown me before the monster comes?" she asked.

He shook his head.

"If you really want to help me, untie these knots."

He shook his head again. "My father would kill me."

Just what I'd like to do, Hippolyta thought. She wondered why Tithonus was there if he didn't mean to help her.

"Then go back to your palace," she said, "and think about your . . . *sister*"—it was hard to say the word, but she managed—"being ground to little bits between the teeth of a monster."

He shuddered, and his head drooped guiltily. "You must be very afraid."

Hippolyta didn't like the way his pity made her feel. "I'm an Amazon warrior," she said. "I'm not afraid to die."

Tithonus glanced over his shoulder at the waves, still crimson with the sunset. "I would be."

Hippolyta made another futile tug at her bonds. "You're only a little boy. *And* a Trojan." She said the eight words with as much contempt as she could muster. "But if you're not going to free me, why have you come?"

"To ask you about my mother," Tithonus said, his voice on the edge of a whimper.

"*Our* mother."

He nodded. "But maybe you just want me to go. So you can die in peace."

"No," Hippolyta said quickly, "stay."

"Do you mean it?" His face seemed to brighten a bit.

Hippolyta nodded, though the effort made her neck hurt. The hours in the sun, arms tied to the pillars, had given her a splitting headache, but she was trying to think clearly. And she was starting to form a plan.

"We can talk a bit. Before dark. Before the monster gets here. But," she whispered hoarsely, "my throat's awfully dry."

Tithonus lifted the waterskin again. It grazed her lips, and water splashed over her face. Shaking off the droplets, Hippolyta cursed.

"I'm sorry," Tithonus said. "I'll try to be more careful."

"Give me the waterskin," Hippolyta ordered. "Put it in my hand." She spread the fingers of her right hand.

"But you won't be able to—"

"Just do it!" She took a deep breath. "Do you want me to die of thirst before we have a chance to talk?"

Tithonus did as she said.

Hippolyta made a great show of trying to stretch her neck and head toward the right to bring herself closer to the waterskin.

"If you loosen the thong just a little bit—not all the way, I know your father wouldn't allow it—then I'll be able to swallow," she said.

Tithonus hesitated.

"Just a little," she wheedled. "Then I'll answer all your questions."

He reached up to where her wrist was lashed to the pillar, plucking at the thongs but to no effect. "I can't do it," he said. "It's tied too tight."

"Try again," Hippolyta urged. It was difficult keeping the desperation out of her voice. She kept thinking that even her little sister Antiope would have worked harder at the knots. "Try again," she whispered.

"I can't."

"Then I *can't* tell you anything about our mother. I won't have the voice"—and she let her voice go gravely—"or the time."

He twiddled with the thong some more, and at last the bond began to loosen. As soon as she felt it give a bit,

Hippolyta pulled at it with all the strength she had left.

With one strenuous heave, her right arm came loose, and the waterskin went flying. She smacked her fist into Tithonus' startled face. While he tumbled backward, down the rough stone slope to fall on the shingle below, she loosened her left hand.

Then she began flexing her fingers to get the numbness out and rubbing her chafed wrists. Reaching down for the waterskin, she'd almost picked it up when a roar thundered out of the water.

The sea below her was bubbling like a cauldron, big waves heaving onto the shore. Three gigantic green humps mounded out of the water, and when they plunged in again, a cloud of spume rose high into the air.

Someone screamed.

For a moment Hippolyta thought it was she herself. Then she remembered Tithonus and looked around for him. He was half sitting, dazed and frightened, on the beach, the waves lapping over his feet.

Many different thoughts wrangled in Hippolyta's head:

I could leave Tithonus to the monster.
I could save him and bring him to his father.
We could both be eaten.
I could kill the monster.

But all these were subsumed in one final thought: *I can bring him back to Themiscyra.*

She smiled grimly at the thought. He was a spoiled,

whiny, useless princeling and she didn't like him at all. Besides, his father would have sacrificed her, so she would sacrifice Tithonus in place of the baby. It was the only way left to her, now that Laomedon had refused to help her mother. She would take Tithonus to Themiscyra and give him to Valasca for the altar in exchange for her mother's release. Then there'd be only one live boy child born of Otrere in the world. Wouldn't *that* fulfill Artemis' demands?

Hippolyta looked back at the sea. The dark, humping shapes were above the waves again and heading once again toward the shore.

Tithonus was right in the monster's path.

Hippolyta pressed a knuckle to her mouth to keep from screaming. An Amazon doesn't scream. Then she scrambled down the slope to rescue the Trojan prince.

CHAPTER THIRTEEN

PREY

H ippolyta was glad of her sturdy leggings as she slid and scrambled over the shards of flint that covered the sharp incline. She hit the shingle with a wet thud, and Tithonus cried out.

She touched his shoulder. He cried again and turned, saw her, and whispered, "Mother?"

"I'm not your mother!" she whispered hoarsely. "I'm your sister—worse luck!" She saw that his eyes were partly glazed, and he seemed unable to focus. His head fell backward and his eyes closed again.

Nervously she glanced out to sea and saw the water seethe and swell. A huge submerged shadow was drawing nearer to the shore. There was no time to be nice to the boy.

She slapped him.

His eyes fluttered open again, then closed.

She slapped him harder.

"What—" he began.

She dragged him up by the arm, and he seemed to wobble about.

Hippolyta bit her lip. If she couldn't wake him up, she'd have to carry him. But before she picked him up, she quickly looked around the narrow stretch of beach.

There was nowhere to hide. High crags blocked them on both sides. Either she ran straight back up the flinty slope, or . . .

"Prince," she said sharply.

He barely registered her voice.

"Tithonus!" She tried again.

He tried to look at her.

"WE'RE GOING TO BE EATEN BY THE MON-STER!" she yelled.

This time he heard.

"Follow me," she said.

She clambered nimbly up the slope, clawing at the rocks and jamming her feet into any holes and crevices to give her purchase on the rocks.

But Tithonus only managed to get two steps up before collapsing. "No use," he cried.

"I agree you're no use," she muttered under her breath. "But I'm not letting that monster eat you. I have other plans for you."

She backed down and grabbed him by the shoulder of his tunic. Then she lugged him up till he was beside her.

"We're both getting out of here," she told him. "Together."

They began struggling up the slope, Hippolyta dragging Tithonus along every few feet. It was hard work, and they were both sweating profusely, but they made the top of the slope before the shadow of the monster reached the shore. Their fingers were scraped raw, and Hippolyta's arms, already aching from the long hours she'd spent tied up, now hurt from hauling the boy.

When they reached the top, they collapsed facedown on the rock.

Then Tithonus gave a strange squeak, and Hippolyta turned and looked at him over her shoulder. He was pale and shaking and pointing his hand at the sea.

One great green coil was rising high out of the sea, throwing off tons of water that crashed as waves against the shore.

Then something big as a boulder broke the surface: the monster's scaly head, with unblinking serpent eyes. When the mouth yawned open, Hippolyta saw row upon row of daggerlike teeth. She'd never seen that many teeth on a creature before.

"It—it—it looks hungry," Tithonus whispered.

"It can stay that way!" Hippolyta told him. She jumped up and pulled him up with her. They leaped off the rock face, then began to run frantically across the stunted brown grass.

"My chest hurts," Tithonus wheezed.

"I know a cure for that," Hippolyta said.

"Really?"

"Being eaten." She shoved him ahead of her and then made the mistake of looking behind.

The monster's head had just cleared the rim of the headland. Giant claws, like great bronze clamps, dug into the broken ground as it hauled its long body out of the sea.

"Faster!" Hippolyta cried, pushing the boy again.

This time he tripped and fell, and Hippolyta bit back the curse that filled her mouth. If he'd been training in Themiscyra, the instructors would have thumped and sworn at him for his weakness.

"Run, Tithonus," she hissed at him, "And I promise you'll see your mother."

He tried to run faster, but she knew he was much too slow.

She knew *she* was much too slow.

Glancing back again, she saw the whole of the monster was now on the land, its ungainly body perched on four stubby legs that propelled it forward awkwardly. Its neck had stretched out the entire long length; the gaping mouth hissed horribly. Its feet thumped the ground like hammers, and its tail lashed from side to side.

The question, Hippolyta knew, was not how fast could they run, but where could they go?

Then, cresting a small rise, she saw a farm ahead of them, a cluster of battered buildings leaning on one another like old friends. Perhaps they could hide—

"There!" she cried, pointing.

Tithonus tried to say something but hadn't the breath, and Hippolyta knew that it wouldn't be long before she'd have to carry him or leave him to his doom.

She was certain that the farm was their only hope. They had enough time to get there before the monster was upon them. Enough time for that—but little else.

Maybe there's a weapon at the farm, she thought, which would at least allow her to fight the monster, though the gods knew she'd no desire to get close to its ugly head.

"Artemis," she cried, "if you have any mercy in you at all, now would be the time to let it show!"

Dragging Tithonus by the arm, Hippolyta hauled him into the first open doorway, which led into the farm cottage's single room.

There was a crude table, a broken chair, and a back exit guarded by a tattered cloth instead of a door. The roof to the cottage was gone and the evening sky hung over them.

The air around them suddenly grew heavy and smelled of the bottom of the sea.

Tithonus looked up and screamed.

Hippolyta knew that the creature had found them. "Run!" she cried, dragging him with her through the tattered curtain and out the back.

No sooner had they left the cottage than the monster brought its whole weight down on the little building, demolishing it in an instant. A cloud of flying rock and plaster filled the air, and Tithonus was knocked onto his knees.

Hippolyta yanked him up, hurriedly glanced around, and saw their one chance for survival. "The well," she cried.

The boy could scarcely move, so she had to drag him over to the well. There was a ragged rope hanging on the other side, but they hadn't the time to get it. The monster was already upon them, and his breath stank of fish and flesh and other things too awful to name.

"Jump!" Hippolyta croaked, and leaped over the edge of the well, dragging Tithonus with her.

Above their heads the colossal jaws crashed shut like the sound of trees breaking in a storm.

Hippolyta caught her breath as she hit the water fifteen feet down. She was plunged into a cold dark, and the waters closed over her head.

The River Styx, she thought as she sank, *the river that runs around the Underworld, would not be this cold.*

Then her feet touched the slimy bottom of the well, and she pushed against it and propelled herself up again. When she broke the surface of the well water, she flailed around for something to hold on to. After a moment her fingers found the rope and the clay jar that had been used for bringing up water.

Tithonus too broke the water's surface, and before he could sink again, she grabbed the braided collar of his tunic and pulled him close.

Just then the monster stuck its snout into the well's top. But its head was too big, and it could not force its way down. In frustration it roared and roared, and the well's echo nearly deafened them. Hippolyta fought the urge to put her fingers in her ears and instead hung on to Tithonus with one hand, the clay pot with the other.

The monster gave one more awful roar, then stomped away.

"Thank you, Artemis," she whispered.

"I'm freezing," Tithonus said. Indeed his teeth were chattering.

"Just a few minutes more, till we're sure that monster's gone," Hippolyta said. "Then we'll climb the rope out of here." She looked at Tithonus, who was now shivering uncontrollably. "You *can* climb a rope, can't you?"

He nodded.

She wondered, though. Exhausted, frightened, cold, even she was going to have trouble climbing.

"You'd better go first," she said. "I'll be behind you all the way."

CHAPTER FOURTEEN

COMPANIONS

They crept out of the farmyard under the light of a full moon, thankful to find the sea monster no longer around.

"Gone to find easier prey," Hippolyta said to the shaking boy.

His teeth were clattering so hard he couldn't answer, though he nodded silently.

"Good boy," she told him. "Now let's find some rocks where we can hide out. Our clothes will dry as we walk."

He nodded again.

"And perhaps the serpent, satisfied with what it finds elsewhere, will go back to the sea for a while."

He smiled briefly.

She smiled back.

Neither of them gave a thought to the monster's other prey but stole quickly and gratefully away from the farm.

When Hippolyta awoke in their nest of rocks, morning sun blazing overhead, Tithonus was gone.

She was immediately seized by a sense of alarm and reached for her weapon. Then she remembered she had none.

"Tithonus!" she hissed in an urgent whisper, then listened hard for an answer.

She was greeted by silence.

Cautiously she eased her way out of the small cave into the full glare of the morning sun. There, on the plain below the rocks, was a small figure kicking disconsolately at a stone.

Hippolyta checked all around. There was no sign of anyone. And no sound of any monster. She sighed with relief. Then she clambered out of the rocks.

The noise she made surprised her. Even more surprising was that Tithonus had gotten out earlier and she'd heard nothing.

A warrior, she reminded herself, *never sleeps.*

She bit her lip. She had not acquitted herself well. The monster hadn't been slain. Her prisoner had escaped. Well, at least he hadn't gone far.

She hurried down the rocky slope, calling his name.

This time he heard her and looked up with a faint smile.

"What are you doing out here?"

He shrugged. "Looking for food." Then he paused. "I haven't found anything. And I was . . . afraid to go too far. In case . . . you know."

She *did* know but didn't want to comfort him. "Well, you won't find loaves of bread and joints of mutton lying around on the ground."

"I'd settle for an apple," Tithonus said. "Even the peel would be something."

"Well, there's a bramble bush over there," Hippolyta said. "We can pick some berries." *And*, she thought, looking around at the scrub and brush, *there's always nettle soup.*

The bush was small, and the berries were mostly unripe. Neither of them felt any less hungry after their meager breakfast. The waterskin had been lost back where Hippolyta had been staked out. She didn't suggest they return to look for it.

"I'd be having milk and freshly baked bread for breakfast if I were in Troy," Tithonus whimpered.

"I'd *be* breakfast if you were in Troy," Hippolyta said. Not that she was thanking him. He hadn't meant to help her escape.

"I'm starving!" said Tithonus, paying no attention to her reply.

"Well, why don't you run off home?" she said, adding quickly, "Of course I wouldn't risk it in your place."

That got his attention. He looked at her with wide-open eyes. "You wouldn't?"

"Surely your father knows by now that you set me free with the monster stomping about the countryside."

His lower lip turned down. "That was an accident."

"I know that. You know that. Who else would believe it?"

He looked at his feet, the sandals scuffed and filthy. "My father wouldn't." The stuck-out lower lip now began to tremble.

"I mean," Hippolyta went on, hoping she wasn't slathering it on too thickly, "*I* only ruffled his tunic, and he had me trussed up for monster food."

"But I'm the heir to the throne," Tithonus whispered.

"Don't forget he has another heir now," Hippolyta said. "Little Podarces. The baby I delivered to him. That makes you as expendable as I am."

He looked so stunned and lost that for a moment Hippolyta felt sorry for him. Then she reminded herself what a spoiled brat he was and how she meant to make him suffer. And his father.

"So you have no choice, really," she added.

"What do you mean?"

She smiled and held out her hand. "You have to come with me. To my home. To Themiscyra."

His lower lip snapped back, thinned out. His mouth

was like a sharp, hard line. He looked just like his father. "I thought Amazons didn't let men into their country."

"You'd have to come as my slave, of course," Hippolyta said, furrowing her brow as if in thought. "That way you'd be safe."

"I'm nobody's slave," Tithonus said. "I'm a Trojan prince."

She shook her head. "Not in your father's eyes. In his eyes you're a traitor. And"—she raised her hand, palm out—"I saved your life." Her voice was as stern as any Amazonian teacher. "By the laws of the gods, your life now belongs to me."

He groaned. "Is that true?"

"Absolutely," Hippolyta said. "Why should I lie to you?"

He couldn't think of an answer. She let him try.

At last Tithonus whimpered. "But my mother will set me free, won't she?"

"I expect so," Hippolyta agreed, thinking that with any luck their mother would never set eyes on him. *A dagger will set you free on Artemis' altar,* she thought, *and I will save the Amazon nation with your Trojan blood.*

They trekked northward, away from Troy, and around midday came to a stream, where they drank the clear water gratefully.

Hunger was a hard knot in Hippolyta's belly. But

she'd been hungrier. Amazons trained for such long, foodless treks.

Tithonus had been complaining about thirst for hours. But suddenly he grabbed on to Hippolyta's arm, spilling the water from her cupped hands, and pointed.

About thirty yards upstream an old man had emerged from the trees to water his horse. Apart from a few scraggly gray hairs near the nape of his neck, he was completely bald. His beard was cut so close to his face it was just a dark stubble. He wore a crude smock of ragged sacking tied at the waist with a length of rope.

"Do you think it's one of my father's men searching for me?" Tithonus whispered.

"Do you think your father cares enough to look for you?" Hippolyta answered, annoyed not to have seen the old man first. "Besides, that old man doesn't look like a Trojan soldier." She wiped her mouth with the back of her hand and strode off in the stranger's direction.

Tithonus trailed slightly behind.

The old man was leaning on a wooden staff and chewing on a length of dried meat. When he saw them approach, he didn't seem alarmed in the least. Up close he seemed an ancient version of a warrior. Old battle scars ran down both his bony arms, and on the left arm he wore a bronze armlet decorated with the image of a dragon. It hung loosely, as if it belonged to a brawnier arm than his.

Hippolyta halted a few feet from the old man and

raised a hand in greeting. "Goddess's blessings, old one."

"Blessings to you, strangers," he replied in a creaking voice.

"Old man, we salute your age," she added. "Sage you must be to have attained so many years." Indeed he was the *oldest* person she'd ever seen. "Have you something you could share with two hungry travelers in the name of hospitality?"

The old man tipped his head in the direction of the stream. "Help yourself to the water, children. It's provided by the gods."

Hippolyta glanced quickly back at the stream, where the horse was lapping placidly. She noticed what she should have seen before. The horse carried a bulging pack on its back. There was a spear and ax tied there as well.

She looked back at the old man and said with as much humility as she could muster, "It's food we have need of . . . sir."

"What has that to do with me?"

"I think you have enough for yourself and more besides," Hippolyta said. Her hand went automatically to her belt, before she remembered she had no weapon.

"That depends upon the length of my journey, eh?" he countered, with a crooked grin.

Tithonus tugged on the back of Hippolyta's tunic. She shrugged him off.

"And how far is that, old man?" Hippolyta asked.

Tithonus tugged again.

"As far as Troy, though it's no business of yours, little girl."

She took a step toward him, and Tithonus tugged so hard, she turned on him and hissed like a serpent.

"Let him be," Tithonus whispered. "There's something funny about him."

"He's just a little crazy," Hippolyta whispered back. "Comes from being that old."

Tithonus shook his head. "No, Hippolyta. It's more than that. Look at his eyes. They aren't an old man's eyes."

"You're talking nonsense," she said, and turned back.

But now she saw what Tithonus had seen. The old man's eyes had the kind of fiery intensity to them that suddenly reminded her of the bonfires on Amazon hilltops, lit to warn of an approaching enemy. *Maybe*, she thought, *I should go more slowly here.*

The old man smiled at her. There was a gap between his teeth, as big, she thought, as the entrance to the Underworld.

"Why do you carry weapons, sir?" she asked.

"I have fought many battles in my day," he answered. "Battle has been my food and drink." He smacked his lips loudly. "But as I have no further use for this equipment, I'm taking the tools of my former trade to sell at the market in Troy."

"Will you sell them to me?" Hippolyta asked quickly.

He laughed, a harsh, dry sound, like the cawing of a crow. "Of course not. You're only a girl."

She drew herself up. "I'm an Amazon," she said. "A match for any warrior you've ever encountered."

The old man stroked his chin. "I've met quite a few warriors, my dear. Cadmus. Pelops. Erechtheus. Heroes, all."

Tiring of the game, Hippolyta said, "And you were what—their cup bearer?"

Tithonus gasped aloud.

"You've got a sharp tongue, young Amazon." The old man's eyes narrowed. "A sharp tongue but no sharp sword. Who took it from you, I wonder."

Hippolyta bristled and took an angry step forward.

The old man twirled his staff end over end so quickly it would have cracked her across the face had she moved another inch. Hippolyta was shocked at his speed.

"If," the old man said, sounding remarkably like one of her teachers, "if you were the warrior you think you are, you'd never let your anger lead you into an ambush. Or your hunger into a situation you couldn't control."

It was Tithonus who broke the stalemate. He bowed to the old warrior. "Please, sir, might we purchase some food from you?"

The old man laughed and placed the staff end down on the ground. "This one at least has manners."

Hippolyta let out a long breath, astonished that she'd been holding it.

"But what have you to offer in payment?" the old man asked Tithonus.

The boy slipped a cord from his neck. Tied to it was an amulet with a red jewel in the center. "My father gave this to me to celebrate my birthday." He offered it to the old man.

Holding the jewel up to the light, the old warrior smiled. "Wealthy man, is he?"

"He's—"

Hippolyta elbowed Tithonus before he could reveal his parentage. "His father isn't here now. We are. That's a truly valuable jewel. We want food—and the weapons."

"The weapons too!" the old man exclaimed in amusement. "Next you'll be asking for the horse as well." He handed the jewel back to Tithonus.

"Why not?" Hippolyta said. "You won't need him if he's got nothing to carry."

The old man chuckled. "He's more use to me than some ornament."

"Will you trade or won't you?" Hippolyta said impatiently, her voice rising.

"And if I don't? Will you try to take them from me?"

The scorn in his voice goaded Hippolyta beyond

endurance. "Do you think I can't?" she cried, lunging at him.

The old man jabbed the end of his staff into her stomach, stopping her in her tracks. "If you're going to challenge me, child, you'll need something to fight with," he said, nodding toward the trees, where Hippolyta saw another staff was lying.

"Where did that come from?" Tithonus asked wonderingly.

For a second the old man glanced his way. "Perhaps from the gods, boy."

"More likely you dropped it along the way from sheer carelessness," Hippolyta said.

The old man shrugged. "How it got there doesn't matter. Either way, will you try your skill against an ancient warrior or not?"

"If I win, you'll give us the horse and all it carries?" Hippolyta asked.

The old man squeezed his lower lip between two fingers. "You drive a hard bargain, young Amazon. Well, so do I. If you lose, you must carry my baggage all the way to Troy for me."

"That's ridiculous. I'm no beast of burden," she cried.

"Nevertheless, those are my terms," he said. "Are you afraid to accept them?"

"Afraid? Never! An Amazon is not afraid of anything. Not even death. Especially not death." As she spoke, she remembered her fear of the evening before. Of the serpent's awful head, of the panicked run into the farmyard, the jump into the well. Then, awash in battle fire, she forgot all fear, strode to where the second staff lay on the ground, and snatched it up.

CHAPTER FIFTEEN

THE FIRE OF COMBAT

"**B**e careful," Tithonus whispered behind her.

The concern in his voice irked Hippolyta so much she pushed him aside rudely. Then she walked back to where the old warrior stood and planted herself firmly in front of him.

"Now, old man," she said, "that we're both armed, perhaps you will treat me with respect."

He chuckled, a sound like rushing water over stone. Little water. Large stone. "All you need to do is knock me down to win, Amazon." The way he said the last word was not a compliment. "Then you will have proved yourself worthy of me."

"Worthy of *you*?" Hippolyta felt her cheek flushing.

Yet she willed herself to be calm, counting silently as she'd been taught. Taunting one's opponent was always the opening gambit of any fight. If the old man really had been a warrior, he would know that well. "You think a lot of yourself."

"With good reason," the old man said softly.

Then, with a sudden movement, he twisted his arm, and his staff lashed out at Hippolyta's face.

She jumped back and felt the wood just brush her nose. "You're slow, old man." Holding her own staff horizontally, she fell into a crouch, ready to ward off another blow.

He stepped back and leaned casually on his staff, then picked at his yellow teeth with a casual finger. "That dried venison is so sticky," he remarked.

The hunger knot in Hippolyta's stomach tightened at the mention of food, and she launched a swift counterattack with the point of her staff. The old man effortlessly beat her attack aside with his own staff, then whacked her across the back as she fell forward. She landed flat on her face.

"Beaten already, eh?" he cried.

Hippolyta leaped to her feet and spat dirt from her mouth.

"I may be an old dog," he said, "but I still have plenty of tricks."

Some trick, Hippolyta thought, but she filed it away in her head for another fight. She let her head hang down as if she were indeed beaten, then charged again without looking.

Once more the old man sidestepped her attack, smacking her across her rear as she went by him. But this time he almost missed.

Hippolyta turned and stood glaring at him, panting, flushed partly with rage and partly with hope.

"You're like an angry dog snapping at chariot wheels," the old man said, this time less like a teacher and more like a smug young fighter. "You don't expect me to stand here and let you hit me?"

Then, without warning, he came at her fast as a viper striking from the undergrowth. His staff jabbed and poked; it swatted and swung with such energy and accuracy Hippolyta backed off as fast as she could. She kept swinging her staff from side to side, trying to protect herself. Finally, she stumbled over an exposed tree root and fell backward onto the ground.

Tithonus rushed toward her, and she waved him off, angrily.

Meanwhile the old man turned his back on her and walked over to the river. He knelt and splashed water on his face, then stood up again.

"Frankly," he said turning around, "I'm disappointed. I thought you'd have more spirit."

Getting up, Hippolyta said, "I've plenty of spirit." She no longer addressed him as *old man*. He hadn't seemed very old when he was attacking.

"Oh, you've got anger enough," the warrior conceded. "But you don't know what to do with it. Fire is your friend when it lights your way. It is your friend when it keeps you warm. But if it burns your house down, what use is it to you?"

"Riddles!" Hippolyta said. She spat to one side, to show her disdain, though her mouth was dry as dust.

"I know what he means—" Tithonus began, stopping when Hippolyta glared at him.

"Your riddles won't protect you," Hippolyta snapped. She understood without Tithonus' help what the old man meant. She'd been reckless in her attacks, letting her anger drive her. She'd been too eager to strike him down without sizing him up first, without remembering all her fighting techniques.

She rehearsed them in her head: *Don't let your guard down. Probe your opponent for weaknesses. Watch how he moves.* How could she have forgotten?

When she closed with the old warrior this time, she watched with care, calculating the way he used his staff. She checked his feet out of the corner of her eyes.

There! He took a step forward, signaling an attack.

Now she could sidestep his thrust.

Whack! She struck him a glancing blow across his bony shoulder.

He hopped away, grimacing.

"That must have hurt," she said. "Old bones have little padding."

He flashed her a fierce grin. "That's better, girl. Now we'll really test your mettle."

He came at her faster than she expected. She blocked high, but he swept his staff low and scooped her feet out from under her. She landed hard on her bottom but leaped up again before the pain could keep her down, aiming a blow at his head, then his knee, then his belly. Not one of the blows connected, but the attack was furious enough to get him to retreat, huffing and puffing, like an old boar in a fight for its life.

"There!" he cried out. "Now your blood is flowing, like a river in spate. And you're finally using your speed and your strength, instead of simply squandering them."

Their staffs cracked together, again and again.

Hippolyta had risen above her anger. She was high on battle fever, using it to fuel her ferocity and drive herself on. She repeated the moves she'd practiced since she was a little girl. But now she was putting a passion into each strike that she'd never had before.

An Amazon battle cry burst from her lips. *"Aeeeeeeiiiiiii!"*

And then she was whipping the staff around the old man like lightning in a summer storm. At last she cracked him across the bald skull, and he toppled like a felled tree.

At once the battle fury left her, and she stood, panting, waiting for him to rise.

Tithonus knelt over the old man.

"Is he—" Hippolyta whispered, "is he alive?"

"I don't know," Tithonus said, looking up at her. "But I can't see a mark on him."

Just then the ancient sat up and rubbed his head. "That was good," he said, oblivious of the boy's astonished face. "Very good." He found his staff and used it to stand.

Tithonus stepped away, but Hippolyta held her staff ready. She had no energy left, though. She wondered if she could fight any longer.

The old man looked at her. "Took you awhile, girl." His head nodded up and down, like some sort of addled stork. "But in the end you fought like a warrior. Take your reward, but don't forget the lesson that comes with it." He started off into the woodland.

"Sir," Hippolyta called after him, "you haven't told me your name."

The old man turned back slowly. For a long moment he seemed to be studying Hippolyta's face, as if memorizing it. "I'll tell you that next time we meet," he called. "But I will tell you this, turn east and north that way"— he pointed—"and you will get home a lot more quickly than you came to Troy." Then he grinned broadly, walked into the trees, and disappeared.

CHAPTER SIXTEEN

THEMISCYRA

Hippolyta dismissed the old man from her mind and started ripping open the pack. Inside were loaves of bread, cheeses, strips of dried meat, fruits and berries, and a skinful of wine.

"He must have quite an appetite for someone so skinny," she mused, biting into a handful of figs.

"I don't like it," said Tithonus. "He gave all this up too easily."

"Easy for you," said Hippolyta, rubbing her bruises. "I paid quite a price."

She tossed Tithonus a loaf of bread, and his hunger immediately overcame his curiosity. Having silenced him as she intended, Hippolyta examined the horse and discovered something tucked under the pack, a double-headed ax. She pulled it out and saw that it was identical in every way to the kind used by the Amazons.

"That'll come in handy," said Tithonus. "We can chop wood for a campfire tonight."

"It's handy for a lot more than that," Hippolyta said.

She turned the ax over in her hand, examining it from every angle. If not for the fact that it was impossible, she could have sworn this was the very same ax she had taken with her from Themiscyra.

Once they had eaten their fill, Hippolyta vaulted onto the horse's back and took hold of the reins. Tithonus gaped at her as if she had just turned a somersault and landed feetfirst on top of a tree.

"Come on," she said, waving him forward. "You're not planning to walk all the way, are you?"

"You mean, we're going to sit up there? But we'll just fall off."

"Don't be silly. I've been riding on horseback since I was younger than you."

"Well, that's all very well for a barbarian, but civilized people ride in chariots."

"I know one civilized person who's going to be trampled under these hooves if he doesn't get over here," Hippolyta said.

Tithonus came forward reluctantly and took Hippolyta's hand. She pulled him up with a grunt. It was like dragging up a sackful of vegetables.

"And this is safe?" he asked, his voice trembling slightly. She wasn't certain if he was shaking from fear, cold, or the fact that the horse had started to prance about with an uncertain rider on its back.

"Yes, it's safe. Just put your arms around my waist."

Tithonus threw both arms around her and held on so tightly, she could hardly breathe.

"Try to relax a bit," Hippolyta said. "We aren't exactly galloping. Yet."

Tithonus slowly loosened his hold, but every time the horse made an unexpected movement, he squeezed Hippolyta so hard she gasped out loud.

"This is going to be an awfully long trip," Hippolyta muttered.

Behind her, his head resting on her back, Tithonus nodded.

Remembering what the old man said about going home, she turned the horse's nose east and north. If it got her home sooner, she'd say a prayer for the old man's safety.

It turned out that Tithonus was more trouble than baby Podarces had been.

Yes, he could feed himself.

And wash himself.

And he didn't need to be changed.

But he wouldn't shut up.

All day long he asked endless questions. Hippolyta gave him as many answers as she could stand, all the while avoiding the full story of why she had come to Troy.

"What does Queen Otrere look like?"

"She has copper-colored hair and large amber eyes. Like you."

"Not like you, though."

"No, I probably look like my father."

"I don't look like *my* father," Tithonus said. "That's why he hates me."

"He hates you?"

"Well, he doesn't exactly hate me. But he doesn't like me, either. Do you think *she'll* like me?"

"I don't know. I expect she'll like you as much as I do."

He chewed on that for a while. Then he started up again.

"What are the Amazons really like?"

"Like warriors."

"All of them?"

"Yes."

"Then who does the washing?"

"We have servants. We have slaves."

"Is my mother a warrior?"

"She's a queen. But not the warrior queen. The peace queen."

Another one to chew over.

When he finally stopped asking questions, Hippolyta was relieved.

But only for a moment.

Then he began talking endlessly about Troy: about his father, his sisters, his old nurse, Dares, the stories he'd heard the bards sing at the palace.

Hippolyta tried to keep a rein on her temper, but when he started talking about how soft his bed was in Troy and how many servants he had, it was more than she could take.

"Tithonus," she said through gritted teeth, "if you don't close your mouth, a woodpecker will fly in and make its nest there." It was something her mother often said to Antiope.

"That's silly," Tithonus answered. "There are no woodpeckers around here. There are no trees."

"Then if you don't shut up, I'll find some other bird and stuff it in there!" Hippolyta threatened.

The boy fell silent for a full three seconds, then said, "I think we should stop and rest for a while, Hippolyta. All this riding is making you cranky. I knew we'd have been better off with a chariot. A person doesn't get cranky in a chariot."

"A person does who's tied up and carted off to be a

monster's dinner," she said in a tight voice.

That quieted him.

Hippolyta had to fight hard to stifle her desire to shove him off the horse and leave him lying in the dust. *Let him try to find his way back to Troy without being eaten by a bear,* she thought. *Let him try to get there without being taken by brigands!*

But each time she felt that way she reminded herself that she needed him as much as he needed her.

"It's getting dark," she said finally. "We might as well stop for the night."

She showed him how to gather kindling for the fire, and he took to the task eagerly, as if it were some sort of game. He did such a good job she even let him strike a spark from the two pieces of flint she found in the old man's pack.

"Stay here," she commanded. "Watch the fire and the horse."

She was so relieved to be away from him for a little while she almost missed the trio of pigeons with the makeshift bow she'd fashioned for herself. In fact she only got two of them.

But two, she thought, *are enough.*

Once they'd eaten, Hippolyta lay back on the brown grass. It was the most relaxed she'd felt in days.

"I think food tastes even better out-of-doors," said Tithonus. "When I get back to Troy, I think I'll go outside to eat instead of having my meals in the banqueting halls."

Let him dream about his banquets, Hippolyta thought. *He's never going to see Troy again.*

"My father likes having huge banquets," Tithonus recalled, "with six or seven courses. And music. And dancing girls."

"Yes, I'm sure he has plenty of *dancing* girls," Hippolyta remarked disdainfully.

"You don't like my father, do you?" Tithonus said.

"Do I have any reason to?"

"I suppose not." He said it carefully. Then burst out with "But what about your own father? The one you look like."

"Amazons don't care about their fathers," Hippolyta replied brusquely. "In fact I don't even know who he is."

"Then how do you know you look like him?"

"I don't. I just know I'm the only one of Mother's daughters who doesn't look like her."

"Don't you want to find out who your father is?" Tithonus' voice fell to a whisper, as if afraid to even ask the question.

"Well, I know it isn't Laomedon," Hippolyta replied tightly. "Because he said he'd met my mother only twice. That's once for you and once for baby Podarces."

But Tithonus wouldn't let the matter rest there. "Do you think your father might be a king, though?"

She sighed and turned over onto her stomach. "What

does it matter if he's a king or a commoner? He's just a man—and all of *them* are alike."

"That's not true," Tithonus said thoughtfully. "I don't think I'm anything like my father. He likes ordering people around and fighting wars. I'd rather stay home and listen to the storytellers. I don't think I want to be king if it means fighting."

Hippolyta thought: *I should just tell him he needn't worry about becoming king. That would shut him up.*

"It's late, Tithonus." She yawned. "Get some sleep. You can start talking again in the morning." She flipped over on her back, and before he could think of an answer, she was fast asleep.

Two weeks' travel brought them into the land of the Amazons, a lot more quickly than the trip to Troy.

"My country," Hippolyta said, expansively waving her right arm and thinking about the old man's promise. *Go easily and go well, old warrior,* she thought.

"What's that?" Tithonus asked, pointing to the gleaming river winding its way north.

"We call it the River Thermodon," Hippolyta said. But even as she spoke, something troubled her.

"This land of yours is very quiet," Tithonus commented.

"We're a quiet people," she told him.

But he'd put his finger on what had been bothering her. They'd encountered no Amazon scouting parties, no

Amazon hunters, no Amazon travelers for mile upon mile.

The lack of anyone's trailing them or questioning them or greeting them bothered Hippolyta. It was like a sliver of broken nail on a finger: raw and worrying but not actually deadly. She thought about it on and off until they got closer to the city.

When they saw Themiscyra in the distance, there was no one working in the fields.

"It shouldn't be *this* quiet," Hippolyta murmured. She could feel the hairs standing up on the back of her neck, a sure sign of danger in the road ahead. Her fingers stroked the edge of the ax at her side. She wondered: *Could some enemy have swept across our land while I've been gone?* Then she looked again at the countryside but this time carefully.

Unlikely, she thought. There was no sign of a battle. There was no sign of any destruction.

"Maybe there's a festival going on and everybody's stopped working for the day," Tithonus suggested.

"Maybe you're right," said Hippolyta. Strange how she suddenly, desperately wanted Tithonus to be right. "A festival."

But it was not First Planting nor was it Harvesttime. It was not the solstice, either, when the days grew shorter or longer. It could not be a celebration of a new daughter, for when she'd left, no one who was carrying a child had been near term. The Festival of Founding, in which they celebrated Themiscyra's beginnings, was not for many passages of the moon yet.

What other festivals are there? she wondered.

"That would be fun, arriving during a festival," Tithonus enthused.

"Be quiet!" Hippolyta suddenly told him. "Listen."

She thought at first she was hearing the wind keening through the trees. But the trees were still, and there was no wind.

"That's a funny noise," said Tithonus. "What is it?"

"I don't know," Hippolyta replied.

But she did. It was the sound of weeping voices. And they were coming from Themiscyra.

"Well," the boy said, "what do you *think* it is?"

She was afraid to think. She could only act. She urged the horse forward with her heels.

They followed the dirt road until they came to the wall around the city. Surprisingly, there were no sentries at the gate, no one patrolling the palisade.

It's as if the gods had reached down and plucked every Amazon but me from the earth, she thought.

The keening noise from inside the city was louder now and even more unsettling. It was like a wild mourning cry after battle.

The horse began to grow nervous, whinnying and stamping and trying to veer away from the town.

"We'd better get off before he throws us," said

Hippolyta, skinning one foot over the horse's back and dropping down. She turned to help Tithonus dismount. Then she tethered the animal to a post and patted it gently to calm it.

Tithonus shivered. "I don't think it's a festival," he muttered.

Hippolyta didn't respond.

They passed through the gateway and onto the empty, narrow streets. All at once a woman came stumbling out of one of the houses and ran up the street toward them. Her cheeks were streaked with tear tracks; her face was pale and haggard. She was pulling at her hair in a frenzy of anguish as she ran. She'd actually torn out hunks of it, for there were clumps in her hand.

Tithonus darted behind Hippolyta and hid there.

Hippolyta was hardly less afraid than he, but she stood her ground. She thought the woman looked familiar, though she couldn't put a name to her. Perhaps a servant in the palace or some woodworker who'd fashioned a new table for the temple recently.

"Dead, oh, all of them dead!" the disheveled woman wailed, and seized Hippolyta by the shoulders. "What will become of us now?" The woman stared into her face with wide, bloodshot eyes. Her voice shriveled to a husky sob. "Dead. Dead. All of them dead."

Releasing her hold, the woman sank to her knees and buried her face in her hands.

Hippolyta was torn between the impulse to comfort this madwoman and the impulse to run away before the madness took a dangerous turn.

"Who's dead?" she asked. "Is Queen Otrere safe?"

The woman gave no answer but wept into her hands.

"What's wrong?" Tithonus asked in a small voice.

"I don't know," Hippolyta replied. "Stay close to me, and we'll find out."

"I think we should go back," Tithonus said. "While we still can. Listen, Hippolyta."

They both listened. The great keening filled the city and threatened to overwhelm them.

"This is a place full of ghosts," Tithonus cried.

"This is Themiscyra, not Tartarus," Hippolyta said, turning to face him. "Not the land of the dead. Come on, boy. Don't you want to be a brave warrior like your father?"

Tithonus looked down at the ground. "No," he said in a near whisper.

"Then be a brave warrior like your sister," she said, taking his hand. "Like me."

She led him down the street toward the center of Themiscyra. As soon as they entered the main avenue, she felt his fingers tighten convulsively around hers.

Here was where the sound was coming from. Along the road, slumping in doorways, leaning against walls, draped over the fountain unheeding the water in their faces, were scores of Amazons. Like the deranged woman by the gate, these Amazons were wailing, hair unbound, garments disordered and torn.

Again and again the same words recurred like a dirge: "They are dead, all of them dead. What is to become of us now?"

Hippolyta recognized most of the faces, and that only made things worse. Women she had seen dressed for battle or riding boldly off on the hunt were now weak and helpless, their spirits broken by some dreadful calamity.

Was this the promised curse, she wondered, *the result of her mother's refusal to kill her infant son?*

"Let's get out of here," Tithonus pleaded. "This is an awful place."

"No," Hippolyta insisted. "Not until we understand what's going on. These are my people, but at the same time, they aren't. True Amazons would never act like this. We have to find the queen. My mother. Your mother. She'll tell us what's happening here."

CHAPTER SEVENTEEN

THEMISCYRA'S CURSE

he nearer they drew to the center of Themiscyra, the more crowded the avenue became. They were jostled on every side by grieving Amazons, who were too distracted to notice them. The din of the women's lamentations was overwhelming.

"What are they all crying about?" Tithonus asked. "I don't see anybody dead." He was pressed up against Hippolyta's side, and without thinking, she placed a protective arm around him.

"I don't know," Hippolyta said, almost shouting to be heard above the loud sobs. "Maybe they're under some kind of spell."

A sudden dizziness swept over her, and she leaned on Tithonus' shoulder.

"*Oof*," she exhaled. It was as if the unnamed grief engulfing the others had begun washing over her as well.

"What is it, Hippolyta?" the boy asked, looking up at her.

"Must think," she said. "Must remember my purpose." She was speaking to herself as much as to him. But the grief was coming in waves now, a great tide of it. She felt as if she were drowning.

At that very moment a girl her own age slouched down the street, shoulders bowed down with misery.

"Phoebe!" Hippolyta whispered.

"What's a Phoebe?" Tithonus asked.

It was all Hippolyta could do to nod her head in Phoebe's direction. "Her. Barracks mate," she managed to say.

Phoebe was sobbing aloud. The front of her robe was soaked through with tears; her eyes were rimmed with red. She looked as though she'd been crying for days. Perhaps she had.

The thought made Hippolyta shudder, and she clung to Tithonus.

As if the touch lent him strength, Tithonus cried out to the weeping girl, "Phoebe! Phoebe!" His voice cracked as it sang out over the chorus of weeping women.

Hearing her name, Phoebe looked up for a moment and then, still crying, came closer.

Hippolyta reached out and touched her sleeve. "Phoebe," she croaked, "it's me, Hippolyta. What's happened here? Where's my mother? Where are my sisters?"

The girl's chest heaved with grief, and she had to fight to catch her breath. "They came," she gasped. "They killed everyone."

"But—but—no one is dead," Hippolyta insisted, though there seemed to be a stone in her own heart weighing so heavily it hurt to speak. "Who came? Whom did they kill?"

"*They* came. Everyone is dead." Phoebe howled. "All of them. What are we to do now?"

She buried her face in Hippolyta's shoulder and sobbed.

Hippolyta pulled herself away and, still leaning heavily on Tithonus, continued on down the street. It felt as if they'd fallen into a river and he were holding her head above the water. She was grateful to him and angry in equal measure. He seemed unaffected by the grief. The anger kept her from drowning in the grief.

As they neared the center of the settlement, the mournful chorus grew louder still. At last they reached the great square. Here the madness seemed at its worst, for the square was packed from one end to the other with women rending their garments, groaning aloud, and tearing out their own hair.

"They sound," Tithonus said, "like screeching cranes."

Hippolyta had to clench her hands into fists till the nails drew blood. Otherwise she, too, would have been ripping at her clothes and grabbing handfuls of hair from her own head.

On the far side of the square stood the temple of Artemis atop a set of graceful stairs. The temple was a simple stone structure with a domed roof and fluted pillars. Carved into the lintel over the doorway were the symbols of the goddess: bow, moon, bear. A solitary figure, her back to them, waited on the topmost step, eyes turned toward the heavens. The purple border of her royal robe was visible even at this distance.

"Mother!" Hippolyta cried out, astonished to find Otrere out of prison. "Mother, I've returned!"

Her voice was drowned out by the shrill lamentations of the Amazons in the square. Otrere showed no sign of having heard her.

"Is that her?" Tithonus cried. "Is that my mother?" For a moment his excitement overcame his fear. He loosened his grip on Hippolyta and strained for a better view of the queen.

"If anyone here still has her wits, it will be Mother. The guards must have let her out in their confusion," said Hippolyta. "Come, Tithonus."

He grabbed on to her hand again, and she could feel both his eagerness and fear in the sweaty palm. Jostling their way through the mob, they climbed the temple steps till they stood right below the queen.

"Mother!" Hippolyta cried again.

Otrere didn't look around. But this close it was clear that the queen too was affected, for she was praying wildly to the sky.

"Mother," Hippolyta choked out the single word, and then was struck dumb.

At last Otrere turned and looked directly at Hippolyta. Her eyes were reddened, weary; her full lower lip quivered. "Weep, my daughter, weep for us all," she said. "There is nothing left but sorrow now. They are all dead. All. All dead."

Pale and frightened, Tithonus stepped out from behind Hippolyta and went up the steps till he stood next to the queen. He reached out a tentative hand and lightly touched her disheveled hair. She didn't seem to notice the touch or to recognize that there was a boy on the steps of the temple, so lost was she in misery.

Hippolyta started to sink down onto the step when she felt a small hand tugging on her arm. "Hippolyta, Hippolyta, look at me," cried Tithonus. He sounded very far away. "Remember that you're a warrior."

Hippolyta drew a forearm across her eyes, wiping away the tears.

"You saved me from the monster. Remember?"

She took a deep breath to steady herself.

"You took me from the well. Remember?"

She stood on trembling legs.

"You beat the old man at quarterstaffs. Remember?"

She looked at him, though tears still trembled in her eyes. "Yes," she whispered. "Yes, Tithonus, I do remember."

"Then *get us out of here!*"

She looked at Tithonus and saw the expectation in his face. He was trying *his* best to be brave. She would have to try *hers*.

"Yes," she said. "There has to be something I can do."

"There is," said a strange voice.

Hippolyta turned quickly and saw old Demonassa standing in the portico of the temple. There was no trace of grief or distress in her face. Hippolyta was surprised she hadn't recognized the old woman's voice.

"Who's that?" whispered Tithonus.

"The priestess of Artemis," Hippolyta replied. "The one who helped me get your brother to Troy." She was about to address Demonassa when the old woman raised a hand to silence her.

"Always we return to the beginning," the old woman said, gesturing about. "So many lessons must be learned over and over. What was then is now. The past repeats. Arimaspa comes to Themiscyra." Her voice rose easily above the lamentations of the distraught women.

Confused, Hippolyta shook her head. "What do you mean, Demonassa—the past repeats? And what has Arimaspa to do with what is happening here? Is this

Artemis' curse? I thought that the curse was supposed to mean death, but no one here has actually died."

The old woman turned away and pushed open the heavy door of the temple with one wrinkled hand. She waved Hippolyta to follow her into the dimly lit interior.

Hippolyta started forward, and Tithonus was right beside her.

Demonassa looked back and raised a finger in warning. "The boy stays outside."

Tithonus gasped. "Don't leave me alone, Hippolyta," he pleaded.

"Wait here," she said reassuringly. "I'll come back for you very soon. I swear it. Nothing will happen to you here."

Tithonus sank down against the temple wall and pulled his knees up to his chin, as if he were trying to shrink out of sight.

Then Hippolyta followed Demonassa inside, and the door slammed shut behind her. The wind from the closing door made the flames in the little oil lamps dance about. Strange and awful shadows like monstrous winged beings pranced around the room.

Hippolyta began to shake, her hands and shoulders trembling.

"You see what has happened to your sisters?" Demonassa said suddenly, her voice hard. "They brought their queen into my temple to put her on trial for her life. But Queen Otrere's followers came after them, and for the first time Amazons drew their weapons against each other. In here. *In my temple!* And you, child, were the cause of it all."

The old priestess pointed an accusing finger at Hippolyta, and her voice echoed eerily off the temple walls.

"I—I did only what my mother asked me to," Hippolyta responded, "what you asked me to do. To bring the child to his father. How could that be the cause of *this*?" The excuse sounded weak in her own ears. Better to accept the responsibility for her own act than to put it upon someone else's shoulders. She was about to say so when Demonassa stopped her with a wave of her hand.

"Because you thought more of your mother than of me, valued her more than the welfare of the Amazon race, set her word above the laws of the gods, all that you see here in Themiscyra has happened," Demonassa's voice boomed out, and suddenly, as she spoke, she began to change, her features melting and running like candle wax in a hot flame.

Astonished, Hippolyta watched as Demonassa grew younger—younger and taller. In seconds the aged priestess was gone, and in her place stood a young woman whose face shone with a savage beauty. A bearskin cloak covered one shoulder, and pelts and claws decorated her belt. Over her back was slung a bow; a long knife hung at her side. She stared hard at Hippolyta, and her eyes were like the half-moon, filled with darkness and light all at once.

Hippolyta knew her and was afraid. "Artemis!" she gasped, and fell to her knees.

CHAPTER EIGHTEEN

THE GODDESS SPEAKS

Shrugging her shoulders and flexing her sun-bronzed arms, Artemis frowned. "That old woman's shape has left a stiffness in my limbs. Still, the disguise served its purpose. Of all the Amazons, only you know that I am here in your midst."

A tremor ran down Hippolyta's back. It was well known that Artemis spoke to her followers through oracles. But to visit in the flesh . . .

"You do me great honor, goddess," Hippolyta stammered. "I am not worthy."

"No, you're not," the goddess agreed. "None of you are."

Hippolyta swallowed hard, not daring to look up.

Artemis continued. "In times past the Amazons have been my greatest pride, my brave and unconquered warriors. Women of strength and dignity. But look at them now!"

Startled, Hippolyta said, "But wasn't it you who did this to them, Artemis?" Then she bit her lip. How could she be so stupid, to speak that way to a goddess?

Artemis laughed, but there was no delight in the sound. "No, child, not my doing, but my brother, Apollo's. He of the long memory. Years ago, some Amazons wronged him. I had to make a pact to keep him from destroying your entire race. I swore then that should you ever break my laws—and I did not believe such a thing possible—I would see that the Amazons lost all their warrior courage, becoming weak and grief-stricken as in days of old."

"But, goddess, then you admit you . . ." Hippolyta began.

The goddess glared. "Admit? To a mortal? What is there to admit? You Amazons brought this punishment on yourselves. I expected more from Otrere and much, *much* more from you, Hippolyta."

Awed as she was by the goddess, Hippolyta instantly defended her mother. "My mother acted out of mercy," she protested, "mercy for an innocent child." Only after she had spoken did she wonder why the goddess had expected much more from her than from the queen.

She risked a glance up and saw that Artemis was

pacing the floor like a beast caught in a cage.

"Mercy carries a heavy price for warriors. Don't you see that?" the goddess said. "Even now Dares is paying heavily for trying to help you, betrayed by one of his own men. And Laomedon's son will pay more still. Hippolyta, look at your own people. Do you see what they have become?"

"I see it, but I don't understand it," Hippolyta said.

Artemis took a deep breath and seemed to draw all the light of the lamps inside her. Her eyes and skin began to glow. "By breaking the ancient pact, the Amazons have become again what they once were: a helpless band of women. And so they shall remain until this curse is lifted."

"But I thought the curse was about death and this is—" Suddenly Hippolyta recalled Demonassa's saying that the gods always spoke in riddles, never straight on. "This . . . curse. Am I the one fated to lift it?"

"You can try," Artemis said. "But you can do nothing here. The curse can only be lifted in the birthplace of the Amazons, in the lost city of Arimaspa. Find the city, and you find the temple where the first blood pact was made, where women became warriors and cast off the chains of passion and grief that had bound them for so many aeons."

"Is there any chance that I will succeed?"

Artemis laughed again, a short bark of a laugh, without a bit of mirth. "A person's fate is not written in stone by the gods. Only you can write it as you live it."

"Oh," Hippolyta said, not sure whether she was relieved by what the goddess said.

"Come to me."

Artemis' tone of command was so sharp Hippolyta hurried to her side, and the goddess led her to the plain stone altar in the center of the temple.

"Here you offer your tributes to me," said Artemis. "Wine, corn, a kid, or a lamb. And here the second son of your mother should have been offered as well."

"I have brought another in his place," Hippolyta said, wondering why saying it made her feel so awful. "His name is Tithonus. He's also a son of Laomedon."

"He is not an acceptable sacrifice here," the goddess said.

Hippolyta let out a great breath, thinking: *Now we are free of one another, brother.* She was surprised at how relieved she felt.

Artemis gestured down to the altar by her feet. "Do you know what was placed here when this temple was founded?"

Hippolyta shook her head.

The goddess bent down and lifted up the great stone as easily as if it were a mere pebble. Hippolyta caught her breath, and at the sound Artemis smiled. "The things of this earthly world are of no weight to an Olympian," she said, setting the stone aside. "Now look."

Beneath the altar was a stone carving depicting a

swordswoman battling a monstrous winged lion. The monster hovered in the air over the woman's head, grinning with terrible teeth and raking her with sharp talons while she stabbed upward with her sword.

"Do you recognize the beast?" Artemis asked.

Hippolyta shook her head again.

"It's called a gryphon, one of the sacred monsters of Apollo."

"What has this gryphon to do with me?" Hippolyta asked.

"Mortal memories are so short," said Artemis scornfully. Sparks of light flashed like stars in the midnight of her hair. "And mortal minds so foolish."

Hippolyta suddenly remembered what her mother had told her about the gods. That sometimes the only way to get their attention was to make them angry.

"Perhaps we mortals wouldn't be so foolish if you didn't hide so much from us," she said.

Artemis swung around and fixed her with an awful gaze. Hippolyta's heart was pounding, but she stood firm. If Artemis decided to put an arrow through her heart, trying to run away wouldn't do much good.

Instead of a punishment, Artemis smiled. "You're a true Amazon indeed," she said. "The daughter of greatness. There may be hope yet for your people. But for that you must go to Arimaspa."

"I don't know where Arimaspa is," said Hippolyta.

"No, I don't expect you do." The goddess chuckled

and folded her arms. "Arimaspa lies to the north and east, beyond Colchis, at the foot of the Rhipaean Mountains." As she spoke, Artemis stared at the far wall of the temple, as if she could see right through the stone all the way to those far-off peaks.

"It could take me weeks to get there," Hippolyta objected. "What will become of my people in that time? They can't live like this. They haven't the spirit even to feed themselves."

Artemis turned and looked down at Hippolyta. "I'll sustain them, even in their grief. But only for as long as it takes you to make your journey."

"Thank you," whispered Hippolyta, thinking there was something more she needed to ask and not knowing what it was.

"Take the sacrifice with you," the goddess said. "He will be needed in Arimaspa."

Hippolyta gasped, lowered her eyes for a moment, and when she raised them again, Artemis was gone.

For the longest time Hippolyta could not move. Her mind was no longer full of the tidal wave of grief, but there was a different pain now, like a sharp thorn in her heart.

But at last, as the little oil lamps flickered out one by one, she knew she couldn't remain in the darkened temple. Pushing through the heavy door, she emerged, blinking, into the light of day.

Tithonus was still slumped against the wall. He'd wrapped his arms around his head so that they covered his eyes and ears, blocking off the awful scenes of misery and madness around him. Sitting so still, he looked small and young and vulnerable.

Hippolyta touched him gently on the shoulder, and he glanced up with moist eyes, pathetically glad to see her. "What have you been doing?" he asked. "What's happened to that old woman?"

"She's gone. She was—" Hippolyta checked herself. It would do no good explaining that she'd just been talking to a goddess without sounding as if she'd lost her wits. Besides, she didn't want to explain everything the goddess had told her. Certainly not about the *sacrifice* at Arimaspa.

"We're leaving the city, Tithonus," she said. "Right now."

"Thank the gods!" he exclaimed. "I was afraid you wouldn't come back out and that I'd have to stay here till I died."

Why does he have to talk of dying now? she thought. Her fingers clenched the handle of the ax.

"I told you I'd come back for you," Hippolyta retorted in a brittle voice. "You have to believe what I tell you."

"I do," he answered quickly. "I *really* do. Only when you're afraid . . . it's hard to remember promises." He gulped.

"Well, remember *this:* We're both going to do something to save our mother."

"Mother!" He turned and looked over at Otrere, who was still standing on the top step, looking at the sky. "Can I tell her good-bye?"

"Yes," Hippolyta said. "That's exactly what you should do. And then we'll go."

Tithonus ran back and embraced the standing woman. She was so utterly absorbed in her nameless grief, she was completely unaware of his farewell.

As they rode away from Themiscyra, the boy behind holding on around her waist, Hippolyta thought about sacrifice. *Easier to do it before you know the person's name,* she thought. *Before his face is burned into your heart.*

Then she remembered what Artemis had said. Mercy was a warrior's undoing. If she opened her heart to mercy, it could mean the end of the Amazon race.

"Where are we going?" Tithonus asked.

"To the city where the Amazons began."

"But I should really go back to Troy," Tithonus said. "I have to face Father sometime."

Hippolyta took a deep breath and steeled herself for what she needed to say. She half turned in the saddle to speak to him directly. She owed him that. "Tithonus, I can't make this journey by myself. And Artemis—Artemis' priestess said that it would take both of us to stop the madness in Themiscyra. Both of us to lift the curse that has befallen my people."

Tithonus' face brightened. "Really? You really need *me*?"

Hippolyta nodded. "It's for your mother's—*our* mother's—sake."

Tithonus chewed his lip. "But after we finish at Arimaspa, then I can go home?"

"Yes," said Hippolyta, hating herself for the half lie, for she would only be bringing his body back. "After Arimaspa, I'll take you home to Troy."

CHAPTER NINETEEN

AN ENEMY SOLDIER

Hippolyta urged the horse eastward as fast as it would go. As the animal galloped along, both she and Tithonus fell into the steady, hypnotic rhythm. The sound of the hooves thudding on the grass, the wind in their ears, made conversation difficult.

Tithonus went for whole minutes at a time without saying anything. Mostly when he did speak, he simply asked questions, which he framed in three or four different ways. "Where are we going?" he would say. "Are we going far?" And then: "Will it take long where we're going? What is the name again of the place where we're going?" Then he'd lapse back into a long silence.

Hippolyta ignored him, trying to focus instead on

the tasks ahead. *Arimaspa!* she thought, trying to re-member all that she knew of it.

She knew it was the place where the first Amazon queens had lived. Where a pair of arrogant princes had stolen gold belonging to the gods. She knew the women had left that cursed place and wandered for many years till settling at last in Themiscyra and the other Amazon towns.

But it had been foretold by Apollo that a second son grown to manhood would summon the Amazons to their deaths.

Well, Tithonus was the first son, not the second, and he was not yet full grown.

Artemis had also said that in Arimaspa the first blood pact had been made, and there Hippolyta would make that pact anew.

We can do it, she thought with fierce determination. *We.*

Tithonus and I.

Suddenly she felt as if she had a bronze dagger in her heart.

Would Tithonus understand when the time came for him to be killed? The Trojans had been willing enough to sacrifice *her* for their own city's sake.

Whatever we face in Arimaspa, she concluded, *will be worth it to save my people. Worth it to me, at least.*

She did not want to think about what it was worth to the boy.

Hippolyta decided the best route was to go directly to the southern coast of the Euxine Sea and follow the coastline until they reached the border of Colchis. There they would swing south, skirting the actual country, for the Colchians were a suspicious people. It was said they jealously guarded some great treasure gifted to them by the gods. She smiled crookedly. Rather like the Trojans and their precious statue of Athena.

Two mornings farther along, as they were washing their hands and faces in a cold stream, Hippolyta worked up the nerve to ask Tithonus about sacrifice. Not naming names, of course. Not mentioning the actual ritual to come. Just enough to sound him out.

"Tithonus," she said. His name came out as a croak, and she had to clear her throat to speak properly. "Tithonus, do you think a warrior should be ready to give his life for his city?"

He thought a minute. "Father says so," he replied, shaking droplets of water from his hair. "He's sent a lot of soldiers to do that already." He was silent for a moment. "I don't know what the soldiers thought about it, though."

Hippolyta stood and spoke without looking at him. "Suppose Troy was in some terrible danger," she said, "and you were the only one who could save it, but you'd have to sacrifice your life to do so." As they talked, they walked back to the horse, and Hippolyta busied herself untethering the beast and making it ready for riding.

Tithonus wrinkled his nose. "How could my life save the whole city?"

"Well, suppose an enemy army is approaching Troy because you've made their king very angry." She spoke to the horse, not Tithonus.

"How did I do that?"

"*You* wouldn't find it hard. Trust me." Hippolyta sighed.

He nodded as if he suddenly understood. "Yes, kings get angry very fast. I expect it's because they've a lot on their minds. Wars, taxes, sea monsters."

"Well," said Hippolyta impatiently, "you've made *this* king angry by—by setting fire to his beard."

Tithonus laughed and slapped his leg. "That would be funny."

"Not to the king with the singed beard," Hippolyta said.

"True."

"The point is," Hippolyta persisted, "would you give yourself up to the king to save the city?"

"To save the *whole* city? My sisters and my friends?" Tithonus stared off into the distance as though he were recalling their faces. "And my father and Dares and—"

"*Everyone,*" Hippolyta said firmly. She mounted the horse in one quick, flawless motion, then reached down a hand and pulled Tithonus up behind her.

"Yes, I would," he said at last, into her ear. "If I didn't, it would be like living under a curse for the rest of my life."

Absentmindedly stroking the horse's mane, Hippolyta murmured, "Yes, it would, wouldn't it?"

A week after leaving Themiscyra they passed through a land of low, rolling hills. It was a pleasant land, where plovers danced on the wind and dappled deer could be seen grazing under small trees.

They kept to the back country, and the few times they spotted other travelers in the distance, Tithonus wanted to rush over to find out who they were. But Hippolyta insisted they needed to hide.

"Why?" Tithonus asked. "Why not talk to them? Why not get the news? Why not see if they know where Arimaspa is?" The farther they had gotten from Themiscyra, the more his spirits had lifted.

She turned in the saddle and hushed him with a look. "Because I'm an Amazon, and too many people outside my own land will want to capture me. Because you're a Trojan prince and could be held for ransom. Because it's best that no one knows what's behind the walls at Themiscyra. Just *because* . . ."

It shut him up.

For a little while.

But Tithonus' tongue was loosened now, and he clattered on like a nest of starlings. Whenever they let the horse walk—and the poor beast carrying two could not be made to run at length—Tithonus chattered.

He talked of Troy and its unbreakable walls, of his father and the many rules a prince had to follow. He was just going on at length about his old nurse, Trophima, when he spotted something ahead that made him bite his lip and stop talking.

Hippolyta was so relieved by his lack of speech that at first she didn't notice what had silenced him. Then Tithonus pointed a shaking finger, and she followed its direction.

Lying at the foot of a dry tree, clad in gray drawstring trousers and a badly torn and bloodstained gray shirt, was a dead man. A pleated cloak, once green, now also gray, wrapped his shoulders. His sandals were cracked and old.

Hippolyta reined in the horse and peered down at the still figure.

"There's blood on his arm," Tithonus observed. "And his head."

Hippolyta scanned their surroundings with sharp eyes, looking out to see if whoever had killed the man was lurking in ambush nearby. When she saw nothing suspicious, she urged the horse on. They trotted a good thirty feet past the prone figure.

"Are we just going to leave him?" Tithonus sounded shocked.

"There's nothing we can do for him," said Hippolyta.

"And we've nothing to gain by burying him but the loss of precious time. His clothes are too torn and old for use. Why rob the buzzards of a meal?"

She tried to ride on, but Tithonus reached forward and grabbed her arm. "He moved!" he exclaimed.

Hippolyta squirmed around and looked back. As if to confirm what Tithonus had just said, the wounded man let out a loud groan, and his right arm fluttered.

Immediately Tithonus slid down from the horse and hurried over to the stranger.

"Stay back, Tithonus!" Hippolyta called after him. "It might be a trap." She'd heard of robbers who sometimes pretended to be dead or injured in order to lure travelers into their reach.

But Tithonus paid no attention to her. He was already bending over the stranger and examining his wounds.

Hippolyta gritted her teeth in exasperation and dismounted. Leading the horse, she moved cautiously over to the wounded man, but she kept her hand close to the ax just in case.

Tithonus pulled the waterskin from the horse's pack and took it over to the stranger. He yanked out the stopper and was just leaning over the man when Hippolyta called out, "Ho, Tithonus, that's our water. We need it for our journey."

"We can get more along the way," said Tithonus.

The stranger was trying to push himself up on his

good elbow. He muttered a few incoherent words as Tithonus put the waterskin to his dry lips and let the water trickle into his mouth.

Hippolyta scrutinized the injured man. Clearly he was wounded, but that didn't entirely argue against a trap. *Still,* she thought, *perhaps we can get some information from him, or . . .*

All at once she saw that he'd been lying on a dagger. Now that he was sitting up, it was exposed. She'd seen similar weapons hung up as trophies in the banqueting halls at home.

"Get back!" she growled to Tithonus, raising her ax. "He's a Lycian."

Tithonus didn't look up from his task. "So?"

"He's an enemy of the Amazons."

"Look, he's hurt. We need to help him."

She grabbed Tithonus' arm, spilling a great deal of the water on the Lycian and on the ground. "Help him? I don't think so. You don't know what his people and their leader, Bellerophon, did to us. Hundreds of Amazons were slaughtered by them. The smoke from the funeral pyres filled the sky for days."

"He's not an army, Hippolyta," said Tithonus. "He's just one man."

"Yes, a *man,*" Hippolyta said, suddenly bitter. "My point exactly. Reason enough to leave him to his fate."

"I'm a man—well, almost—and you didn't leave me to my fate," Tithonus reminded her.

"Maybe it would have been better if I had," Hippolyta snapped back at him.

A momentary hurt passed across the boy's face. Then he squared his shoulders stubbornly. "You can't just leave him without helping," he said. "We're not barbarians."

"*I* am," said Hippolyta. "Remember?"

"That was a long time ago," said Tithonus. "You've gotten a lot nicer since then."

The unexpectedness of the remark stung. "Not as much as you think," Hippolyta murmured under her breath.

Tithonus helped the Lycian drag himself to the base of the tree and lean his back against it. Dried blood stained his right arm and temple, and there was a wound in his side that had been hastily bandaged with a torn strip of cloth.

Hippolyta stood over him, hefting her ax threateningly. "You're a long way from home," she noted coldly.

The man looked her over with half-lidded eyes. "Amazon," he said heavily, "it's because of you I'm here."

He stopped to wipe his watering eyes and catch his breath.

"I'm not to blame for your misfortunes," Hippolyta answered scornfully.

"I was guarding a merchant caravan on its way to trade with the Ashuri," said the Lycian. In his weakened condition each word seemed to cost him an effort. "Your raids have made such an escort necessary."

"Nevertheless," Hippolyta said, "it wasn't Amazons who did this to you." *How could it be,* she thought, *when none of them could venture more than a few feet without being overwhelmed by nameless grief?*

"No," the wounded man admitted, "it was the Kethites who attacked us." His face twisted as much with pain as hatred.

"Kethites?" Tithonus looked puzzled. "I've never heard of them."

"Pray that you never meet them, either," the Lycian said, then groaned. "They swept down on us in their great war chariots with all the fury of the storm god they worship. They forge their weapons out of iron, not bronze, and with them they slaughter everyone who stands in their way."

"What's iron?" Tithonus asked.

"A stronger metal than bronze," the man said, coughed, and for a moment was still, as if gathering strength. "A gift from the gods of war."

"So, how did you survive?" Hippolyta asked pointedly. "By running away?"

The Lycian bristled. "I'm no coward, young Amazon." He tried to reach behind and pick up the knife but was too weak to do so. "I was brought down in the first attack and knocked unconscious, left for dead. I managed to crawl away after they fled with their booty."

"And where is the rest of your party?" Hippolyta asked.

But before the man could answer, a dull, rumbling noise made them all look up. A cloud of dust was rising up over the eastern foothills.

The Lycian grimaced in pain. "Only the chariots of the Kethites raise such a cloud," he said, and groaned again. "They'll kill us if they find us."

Hippolyta grabbed Tithonus by the sleeve of his tunic and started to pull him away. "Come on. If we start now, we can be gone before they get here."

Tithonus tugged himself loose. "We can't just leave him." He tried to help the soldier up.

Hippolyta was so exasperated she wanted to punch him. "What are you doing, you stupid boy? The horse can't carry all three of us!"

"Then we'll just have to hide," Tithonus said, trying to support the man's weight by himself and failing.

Hippolyta didn't know whether to leave them both to their fates or whether she should knock the boy on the head and drag him away with her.

"He's the *enemy*!" she howled.

"He's not an enemy of Troy," Tithonus said. "And how can he be your enemy? He can't even walk."

"And neither can you, carrying him!" Hippolyta let out a screech of frustration and kicked the nearest rock so hard the pain shot straight up her leg. The rumbling sound was growing louder by the second, and the cloud of dust was drawing worrisomely close.

She turned and shoved Tithonus aside. Pushing her shoulder under the Lycian's arm, she managed to keep him standing.

"Go get the horse," she ordered the boy. "We'll try to reach those rocks over there." She pointed to a great jumble of gray stone hard against a low hill. Each of the boulders was as large as a temple door. "If we could hide from a sea monster, surely we can stay hidden from a band of Kethite warriors."

CHAPTER TWENTY

KETHITES

"I can't make it."

The Lycian soldier was now panting, and his face glowed with sweat or fever. Hippolyta couldn't tell which. His feet dragged on the ground. It was all she could do to keep him upright. Without his cooperation, she couldn't haul him more than a few inches forward at a time.

"Surely you can get as far as those rocks," she said. "Or are all Lycians really the weaklings they say?"

The man bared his teeth—as much against his own weakness as against Hippolyta—and pushed himself on, leaning heavily upon her shoulder.

"Hurry up with the horse," Hippolyta called to Tithonus. "The Kethites will be in sight any moment."

It seemed to take an eternity, but at last they reached the shelter of the rocks. Hippolyta let the Lycian slide to the ground and took the reins from Tithonus. She coaxed the horse down onto its side as she had been taught years before by her riding instructors. Lying alongside the animal, she laid a hand across its muzzle to quiet its anxious whinnying.

"Keep low," whispered the Lycian, following his own advice. "Kethites are always on the watch for enemies. It's said they have a third eye in the back of their heads. Though I've never seen it, I believe it."

Hippolyta peered cautiously through a chink in the rocks. At first all she could see was a cloud of dust kicked up by a multitude of hooves. Then she could see the vague outlines of horses. As they drew closer, she could see the chariots themselves, and they were like nothing she had ever seen before.

The chariots were bigger and heavier than those driven by the Trojans and were pulled by pairs of huge, powerful horses. Each chariot carried a crew of three, and the axle had been placed in the middle of the chariot instead of at the rear in order to support the weight. One of the crewmen was the driver, another carried a large iron-tipped spear, and the third held a shield large enough to protect all three of them in battle.

"Very impressive," she whispered.

Tithonus squeezed up beside her for a look. "I think they're clumsy," he said. "Our chariots are faster."

"The Kethites don't need to use speed to out-maneuver an enemy," the Lycian croaked. "Not with that armament. Why, those spearheads can rip through a shield as if it were made of papyrus." He was lying flat now on the rocky ground. "The Kethites charge straight into the ranks of their foes, trampling them under the hooves of their horses." A spasm of coughing shook his body, and he clamped a hand over his mouth to muffle the noise.

Hippolyta started, turned, grabbed the handle of her ax. Someone would have to quiet the Lycian!

But immediately she realized that there was no fear the Kethites would hear him. The thudding of their horses' hooves and the rumble of chariot wheels was so loud, it felt as though the earth itself trembled at their passing.

Hippolyta stared out through the chink once again. The Kethite soldiers looked as intimidating as their weapons of war. They had round faces with low brows, heavy jaws, and small dark eyes. They wore high pointed helmets with flaps to guard their cheeks. Metal rings were sewn into their tunics to give added protection.

Hippolyta counted at least thirty chariots by the time the last of them passed. This final one trailed a good fifty yards behind the rest, who were fading into dust now.

"Rear guard," Tithonus whispered.

Hippolyta nodded. Just what she'd been thinking.

"Watch out for that third eye," he added.

The chariot's spearman was staring at the shriveled tree where they'd found the Lycian. He pointed and jabbered in an agitated fashion at the driver, who brought the horses to a halt.

Hippolyta swallowed hard when she saw what had caught their attention. It was the Lycian's bloodstained cloak and the knife.

The spearman leaped down from the chariot and sprinted over to the tree. Laying his spear against the trunk, he picked up the cloak and knife to examine them. He called to his companions in the Kethite tongue and waved his arm around excitedly.

The other two soldiers climbed down to join him, leaving behind the cumbersome shield. Each of them drew a curved sword and examined the ground for further signs of blood. The spearman took up his weapon again.

"They're like hunting dogs who've caught the scent of their quarry," gasped the Lycian, who was now upright and staring out through another chink in the rocks. "They'll not stop until they've tracked us down."

"Shh," Hippolyta hissed at him, thinking that three Kethites were surely more than she could handle. A full-grown Amazon might have a chance against them, but she was still only a girl. Then she thought: *If Tithonus and I get on the horse now and bolt for it, we might have a chance.* Escape was not for herself but because she knew that she was Themiscyra's only hope.

"It's three against three," said Tithonus, trying to control the quaver in his voice.

"A wounded man and a boy—what use are you to me in a fight?" Hippolyta demanded in a scornful whisper.

"A wounded *Lycian*," growled the soldier. "I'm still a match for any Kethite once he's out of his chariot."

Hippolyta glared at him. "A tongue is not a sword," she whispered fiercely. "You're in no condition to defend yourself. And they've found your knife."

She wondered briefly if she could leave him there to be slaughtered and still preserve the honor of the Amazons.

Probably.

Then came the quick, bitter afterthought: *Probably not.*

She licked her dry lips and looked at Tithonus. He had turned pale, but he was trying his best to be brave. The shadows from the rock fell across his head like a battle helmet. "I'm ready to fight," he said in a small voice.

Hippolyta sighed. She didn't have much of a choice.

"We still have the advantage of surprise," she told Tithonus, handing him her knife. "Stay hidden, stay low, and leave this to me."

"If I'm leaving it to you, why did you give me the knife?" he asked.

"In case the Kethite storm god proves stronger than

my goddess of the hunt," she answered grimly.

Pulling out her ax, Hippolyta made ready to move. The Kethites had found further traces of blood and were edging steadily closer to their hiding place, swords upraised.

The Lycian laid a hand on her arm. "You have courage, young Amazon," he whispered. "I'll always remember that."

"I plan to be around to remind you of it," Hippolyta said.

Her heart was pounding, and her fingers trembled. But at the same time a strange clarity came over her. It was how she had felt when she fought the old man by the river, when she finally refused to let her anger guide her but rather took control of it. Now it was her fear she needed to channel into strength and determination.

For a moment longer she watched the Kethites through the chink in the rocks. They seemed to have lost the trail and were standing toe to toe, bickering. Hippolyta waited until the three of them finished arguing and once more bent over the ground looking for fresh signs.

She forced the horse up and leaped onto its back in one single motion. Digging her heels into its flanks, she sent it galloping at the enemy, shrilling a battle cry. "Aieeeeeee!"

The Kethites scarcely had time to realize what was happening before Hippolyta was upon them.

Few nations had the Amazons' skill at taming and riding horses. Trojans, Lycians, Kethites all preferred the chariot. So the three men were unnerved to see an enemy bearing down upon them from the back of a horse. They scattered before her charge.

Hippolyta had spent her childhood on the practice field striking turnips from the tops of wooden posts. Still, she'd never actually fought against a real foe— except for the old man. And he hadn't actually been trying to kill her. Only to subdue her. For a second she wondered if she really had the strength and will for a battle to the death.

Then she remembered her mother, arms upraised and weeping, and she swung the ax. Turnip or head— she no longer distinguished between them. What mattered was the ax in her hand.

And the honor of her people.

"*Aieeeeeee!*" she trilled again, the years of practice pulling her arm easily through its arc. The ax was well weighted and became an extension of her arm, her hand. It sang through the air and split the spearman's helmet, cracking his skull as he turned.

He toppled senseless to the ground, the spear clattering next to him.

The old man's horse was not used to this kind of combat, though. When the ax hit the helmet, the horse began bucking wildly. Desperately Hippolyta leaned over its neck and cooed soft words into its ear, till it settled and stopped trying to throw her. Then she had to get it to wheel about in order to face her enemies. Her only advantage against the Kethites was the horse. And if she couldn't control it . . .

From the corner of her eye she saw a figure dashing toward her. Turning on the horse's back and clinging to its heaving sides with her thighs, she lashed out with the ax again, just in time to deflect the edge of the Kethite's curved iron sword. The weapons clanged harshly together, and the Kethite snarled at her in his rough tongue.

At that instant the horse turned, smacking the soldier across the face with a wildly flailing hoof. He was thrown backward onto the dry earth and lay there unmoving.

Hippolyta gulped in a deep breath. "Good horse!" she muttered, her voice cracking. She patted the beast with a sweaty palm, then wiped the sweat off on her tunic.

She looked around for the third Kethite, the spearman. She spotted him dashing for the chariot. If he got into it, he would have the advantage. And if he got away, he could bring the whole Kethite force down on their heads.

She struggled to control the horse and launched it in pursuit of the man. The Kethite heard the hoofbeats bearing down on him and turned quickly. He raised his sword and jabbed it upward.

The horse shied away from the iron blade, rearing so

suddenly Hippolyta was thrown from its back. She went heels over head, and the ax slipped from her hand. Landing heavily, she felt as if every bone in her body had been jarred by the impact.

Groaning, she tried to push herself up. Through a blur of pain, she could see the horse trotting away toward the rocks. Could see the Kethite closing in on her.

She groped blindly for her knife. Then she remembered: She'd given the knife to Tithonus. Even if she *could* get up, she'd nothing left to fight with.

She heard a strange sound, part growl, part something else, and looked up. The Kethite was standing over her now, sword upraised, a wolfish grin on his face. He was laughing.

"Get away from her!" squeaked a voice.

Both she and the Kethite looked around.

Leaping down from the rocks, Tithonus dashed toward them, the knife in his hand. Behind him came the Lycian, but he barely had the strength to crawl out of the jumble of stone.

Hippolyta tried to gasp a warning to the boy, to order him to run away, but she hadn't the breath to form the words.

The Kethite punched out at Tithonus with the handle of his sword, as if the boy weren't worth the bother of the blade. The blow sent Tithonus tumbling backward, stunned.

Then the Kethite returned his attention to Hippolyta.

With a grin of triumph he held the sword above his head.

Hippolyta raised a futile hand to ward off the attack, but she knew there was nothing she could do. "Oh, Artemis," she whispered, "I have failed my sisters. I have failed you."

CHAPTER TWENTY-ONE

THE STRANGER

As if from nowhere a javelin came whooshing through the air and drove deep into the Kethite's throat. There was a spurt of blood as the man was thrown backward. He was dead before he struck the ground.

Hippolyta realized she had stopped breathing and took a huge swallow of air. Clambering shakily to her feet, she saw the owner of the javelin walking toward her with a confident swagger.

He was a tall, handsome man with a close-cropped black beard and thick black curls protruding from beneath the rim of his helmet. He snatched up his weapon and casually wiped the blood off on the ground.

Hippolyta suddenly felt sick, as if she had to vomit,

as if she, and not the Kethite, had swallowed blood. She turned her head away, but not before seeing the broad grin on the tall man's face.

What kind of warrior am I, she thought, *to be so stricken by the sight of blood? Molpadia would not feel this way. Valasca would not. . . .*

She heard feet pounding on the ground, turned back to see Tithonus run up to the tall man. "That was amazing!" Tithonus enthused. "You must have thrown that spear forty or fifty feet!"

"Oh, I doubt it was as far as that," said the stranger.

Hippolyta walked away from them and plucked up her ax from the ground. "Get away from him, Tithonus!" she ordered.

It was clear from the man's garb and weapons that he was another Lycian and therefore a potential enemy.

"He saved your life!" Tithonus exclaimed. "And mine. Trojans know how to give thanks, Hippolyta. Don't Amazons?"

The stranger raised an eyebrow. "If I had meant *you* any harm, young Amazon, I would have left you to your fate and not bothered to bloody my spear."

"Yes, that's true," Hippolyta admitted, lowering her weapon. Still, she didn't trust him. *He is too—too—*she thought. And then she had it. *He is too conveniently here.*

Suddenly Tithonus pointed to the wounded Lycian, who had collapsed only a few feet from the rocks. "Can we help him?" Tithonus asked, pointing.

A waterskin was hanging from the stranger's back, and he gave the bag to Tithonus, who splashed a few drops on the wounded man's face to revive him. The Lycian's eyelids fluttered open, and when he saw first the boy and then Hippolyta, he smiled grimly. "So you triumphed without my help."

"Oh, we had help," Tithonus told him, wide-eyed. "From this man here."

"Polemos is my name," said the stranger.

"He's one of your countrymen," Hippolyta added unnecessarily.

"A Kethite was about to finish off Hippolyta when Polemos killed him with a javelin," said Tithonus, his voice filled with boyish enthusiasm. "Sixty feet at least! I've never seen a throw like it!"

Polemos knelt by the wounded man and unwrapped the bandage. Carefully he washed the wound, then produced a mixture of leaves from a bag that hung from his belt. Placing these over the wound, he fixed a fresh piece of cloth on top of it.

"The Kethite weapons do terrible injury," he murmured to himself as he inspected his work.

"If these two hadn't helped me, the Kethites would have finished me for sure," said the wounded Lycian.

"That was nobly done," said Polemos approvingly. He smiled at Hippolyta, who felt uncomfortable receiving such friendly treatment from a man she barely trusted.

She grunted in response.

But Tithonus grinned. "She *is* noble, isn't she? She's the daughter of a queen. And *I'm* her brother."

Polemos looked suddenly grave. "I didn't know Amazons had brothers."

"Some do," said Tithonus with equal gravity.

"Well, then, you're fortunate in your sister," Polemos told him.

"And she's fortunate in me," Tithonus said, his open face wreathed in smiles. "I saved her from a sea monster."

"Did you now?" asked Polemos.

"Well, we sort of saved each other," Tithonus admitted.

"Then I suppose you and your sister will wish to continue your journey now." Polemos spoke directly to Tithonus, but somehow Hippolyta felt he was really addressing her. She was reluctant to answer. He knew too much already.

"Tithonus!" she said sharply. "We're going."

Polemos looked to where Hippolyta's horse was darting about, still spooked by the experience of battle. He let out two sharp whistles, and the animal came running up to him as though it had known him all its life. He stroked its flank with a brawny hand, gently calming it.

"In time he could become a fine war horse, if you treat him well," he said. This time he addressed Hippolyta directly.

"I've had him only a couple of weeks," Hippolyta said. "I got him from—"

Before she could finish the sentence, she realized for the first time that Polemos was wearing a bronze armlet decorated with a dragon, just like the one the old man at the river had worn.

"I got him from an old man," she said carefully. "He wore an armlet just like that." She pointed to the Lycian's left arm.

"They're common enough," said Polemos with a shrug.

Too convenient, she thought. *And too humble by half.* She remembered how skillfully Polemos had thrown the javelin.

"Are you a pupil of his?" she asked suspiciously.

Polemos laughed. "Perhaps I am. If so, I've learned many things in his company. Among them was never to make a man my enemy if he would be my friend. Hate is a poor motive for battle. It is better to fight in defense of the helpless and the innocent." He cast a meaningful glance at Tithonus.

Hippolyta was sure the man knew far more than he was saying, but when she opened her mouth to speak again, he waved her questions aside impatiently.

"Once the rest of the Kethites make a stop, they're going to wonder why this chariot hasn't caught up," he said. "And those two you knocked out will be waking up shortly. What do you suppose they'll have to say to their friends?"

"Then I didn't kill them?" Hippolyta asked. The awful knot in her stomach began to unravel.

"No, but for some time they're going to wish you had," Polemos said. "First their heads are going to ache like the inside of a volcano. And then they're going to remember that a girl beat them, and their pride will feel as hot as their heads. I'll tie them tight and hide them where their friends won't find them easily. Then my countryman and I will take that chariot back to Lycia." He nodded in the direction of the empty Kethite chariot.

"What about us?" Tithonus asked. "Where should we go?"

"Through the rocks and into the hills," Polemos replied.

"*Through* the rocks?" Hippolyta was puzzled. She'd been certain that the rocks hid nothing more than a shallow cave.

"You'll find a fine trail," Polemos said, "though the way through is too narrow for the Kethites to follow, except on foot. Keep always to the left, and no trouble will come to you, even in the dark. You do know left from right?"

They both nodded.

"Good," Polemos said. "When you come out again, you'll see a range of mountains. Look for the one with the double peak. Go toward it, and you'll find what you're looking for."

"How do *you* know what we're looking for?" Hippolyta asked, once again suspicious.

"Surely you seek your ancestral home. Why else would a young Amazon wander so far, with none of her sisters accompanying her?" said Polemos. "Now go, while there's still time."

In spite of her suspicions, the urgent command in his voice jolted Hippolyta into action. She climbed onto the horse and pulled Tithonus up behind her.

"Good luck," Tithonus called to the two Lycians.

"And to you, young prince," called out Polemos. The wounded Lycian waved feebly.

"May the gods . . ." Hippolyta began softly. It felt strange speaking to any men, let alone two she would normally have considered her worst foes. But Polemos' words—about never making a man an enemy if he would be a friend—suddenly repeated in her head.

"May the gods give you safety as well," she said. Then she kicked the horse lightly with her heel.

"Make your battles few and choose them well," Polemos called after them. "Then fight with all your heart."

CHAPTER TWENTY-TWO

FARTHER ALONG
THE ROAD

They threaded through the dark cave passages with a single torch made from a broken tree limb wrapped with the Lycian's torn cloak. It gave a feeble light that flickered and flickered, ever threatening to go out.

Tithonus talked of nothing but Polemos. "Did you see how he appeared from nowhere to save us? Do you think I could learn to throw the javelin with such skill? How do you suppose he knew so much about this country? He must be a very famous warrior back in Lycia." He went on and on without needing any encouragement from Hippolyta—or getting any.

At last she snapped at him, "I beat two of the Kethites

by myself. I don't hear you talking about what a great warrior I am."

"You were very brave," said Tithonus, abashed. "It's just that, well—"

"That I'm a girl?" Hippolyta suggested. "A mere woman? You think I should be busy in the kitchen or weaving a tapestry or prettying myself with makeup and jewels?"

"I didn't say that," mumbled Tithonus, fidgeting behind her uncomfortably. "It's just that men already do enough fighting. If all the women became warriors as well, there would be nothing but fighting all over the world. It would go on and on until everybody was dead."

"Then let the men give up their weapons and leave the fighting to the women," said Hippolyta. "Try *that* idea on your father."

"If I ever see him again," Tithonus said, sighing wearily. He put his head against her back.

Just as he spoke, the torch gave a final sputtering bit of light and went out. The cave was suddenly as black as a tomb.

"If I ever see *anything* again," Tithonus whispered fearfully.

"Don't worry. You'll be at home with your family again," Hippolyta said. Even as she spoke, she hated herself for the half lie.

"I hope so," he whispered.

But Hippolyta suddenly understood. All of Tithonus'

talking had helped him keep his spirits up. But now that they were in the pitch black, he'd run out of both conversation and courage. Now he was only a little boy in the dark.

And he was afraid.

So am I, she admitted as she tried to see something— anything—in all that black.

She dismounted.

"What are you doing?" Tithonus cried. "Don't leave me, Hippolyta."

"I'm not leaving," she said. "But I'm going to have to lead the horse so it doesn't knock itself out walking into stone. I'll keep a hand on the cave wall, and that way we'll know which way we're going."

"All right." Tithonus didn't sound convinced. "But why can't I walk with you?"

"Because you'll be safer on the horse," she said.

Her hand trailed along the wall, which surprised her by being both cold and damp. At the first real crossroads, the horse started naturally to the right.

"Left!" Tithonus cried. "Polemos said we have to go left."

Hippolyta yanked the reins leftward, and the horse reluctantly obeyed. But as they passed by the passage on the right, Hippolyta saw hundreds of bright spots, like eyes, winking at her. She shuddered, hoping that Tithonus hadn't seen them.

"Left it is," she said. "Good thinking, Tithonus."

"Thanks," he answered. There was a bit of lift in his voice.

Lucky he can't see how hard I'm hugging the left wall, Hippolyta thought, *or he wouldn't be so happy.*

She was extra careful after that always to pull the horse to the left. If there were other bright, waiting eyes down the right-hand turns, she didn't want to know.

After what seemed like days, but was probably only hours, they emerged out into a gray afternoon, and Hippolyta quickly remounted and looked around. A fog sat heavily on the shoulders of the mountains around them, like a shawl on an old woman, so she couldn't tell which mountain had the double peak.

The horse brought them into some sort of meadow where the ground was cracked and the vegetation sparse and brown. It began to crop what grass remained.

"We'll camp here," Hippolyta said, gesturing around them. "We don't dare go on in any case, not until we can see which mountain is the right one."

She left Tithonus guarding the horse and circled the meadow slowly but could find only a single twisted tree, some sort of ancient olive. Circling back to the horse, she took the reins from the boy and led them both over to the tree, where she tied the horse.

"Can I sit?" he asked, pointing to the tree. Without even waiting for her answer, he flopped down and sat with his back to the gnarled trunk. He didn't speak a word after that but just stared up at the fog-shrouded mountains. His face was the color of the fog, and he was very quiet.

It rained that night, a heavy, cold gray downpour. They took what shelter they could under the olive tree, but it offered them little comfort, and they were soon soaked through.

In the morning Tithonus was feverish. Hippolyta had to lift him onto the horse, then jump up behind and hold him in her arms. When he leaned back against her, she could feel the heat of his fever through her tunic.

A mountain with a double peak was now clearly visible on the far horizon.

"Just like Polemos said." Tithonus rubbed watery eyes. "He knows everything, Polemos." Then he sneezed three times in rapid succession, each sneeze shaking his thin body.

"I don't like it," Hippolyta grumbled. "I don't like *him*."

"Polemos?"

Hippolyta didn't answer. Instead she leaned to one side and looked back.

"What's the matter?" Tithonus asked, sneezing twice more. "Do you think he's following us?"

"I don't know," Hippolyta replied. "I just have a feeling there's more to Polemos than he showed. He might be behind us. Or he might be . . ."

"Ahead of us?" Tithonus asked.

Hippolyta shrugged.

By the next day Tithonus' cold had gone into his chest, and he was too ill to travel. He coughed now, deep and awful sounds that were almost animal-like. His face was ashen, and tremors ran through his thin body constantly.

Hippolyta built up a fire and wrapped him up as comfortably as she could in her own cloak.

This was a barren stretch of country. Hardly anything grew here, and game was scarce. Leaving the boy to sleep off his fever, Hippolyta went in search of food.

The pickings were small: some tough, bitter roots and a couple of tiny sparrows, which she cooked on the embers of the fire. She fed Tithonus as much as he could keep down and gave him all the water he wanted. She went short herself, knowing that his body needed the nourishment to overcome his illness.

During the night his fever broke, and in the morning he insisted on carrying on.

"Are you sure you're well enough?" Hippolyta asked. She was displeased with herself for being so concerned. *After all, how well does he need to be to be a sacrifice?* she thought.

"I'll manage," Tithonus said, forcing a smile. "I only need to be strong enough to hang on to you."

He stumbled blearily to the horse and waved to Hippolyta to mount up.

Hippolyta could see what the effort cost him and could not help admiring his courage. *Perhaps,* she thought, *it might have been kinder for him if the fever had taken him quietly in the night.*

By the next day Tithonus had shaken off his cold. But they were both hungry and weary of traveling. Since they hadn't found a stream in days, their water was low, and they smelled appallingly.

A bleak northern wind sweeping down from the mountains blew into their faces, and as long as they were riding, they were both chilled to the bone.

Tithonus rubbed his cheeks, trying to warm them. "Why haven't we seen a farm or village?"

"The Scythians who live here in the north are nomads," said Hippolyta. "They're always moving from place to place. So you wouldn't see anything like an actual farm. Or—"

"But we haven't even seen a *camp*," Tithonus said.

Hippolyta had had that same thought hours ago but hadn't wanted to scare the boy. "Well," she said brightly, "who would want to camp here if they didn't have to?"

"You don't suppose there's—there's a monster living around here, do you?" Tithonus' voice was tentative. "A monster scaring off the Scythians."

"We're too far from the coast for there to be another sea monster close by," said Hippolyta. "And we know how to fight off monsters, don't we?"

"But there could be a Cyclops, couldn't there?" Tithonus seemed intent on frightening himself.

"If there is, it should have spotted us by now, even with only one eye," Hippolyta assured him.

"Well, even with *two* eyes, I still can't see any sign of this city of yours."

Hippolyta had to agree. If there were a city below the mountain, they should have seen it by now. And it had to be *below* the mountain. There were too many steep crags guarding the mountain flanks for a city to stand anywhere but directly before them.

"Maybe Polemos lied to us," she said.

"Why would he do that?" Tithonus demanded.

"Because he's a *Lycian*," Hippolyta answered bitterly. "All Lycians are liars."

"That's Cretans," Tithonus corrected her. "All Cretans are liars. At least that's what my father says."

"Unless that's a lie too."

"My father doesn't lie."

"But he doesn't tell you all the truth, or you would have known about your mother."

Tithonus shut his mouth and didn't answer.

The double peak reared high above them now. Other smaller mountains clustered around its slopes like children at their mother's skirts.

"I hope we get there soon," Tithonus said through chattering teeth. "Before I become a block of ice."

"I doubt it'll be any warmer at Arimaspa," said Hippolyta gloomily. She rubbed her hands briskly together, but that generated no real warmth. In fact the only part of her that was even slightly warm was her bottom where it sat on the horse.

"At least Arimaspa will be the end of our journey," he said. "We can lift that stupid curse and go home."

"Why do you want to go home? Remember how much trouble you're going to be in."

He bit his lower lip. "I don't care. I want to see my sisters again and my friends. And my new baby brother."

The reminder of little Podarces stung Hippolyta. "Don't talk about Podarces," she said brusquely. "*He's* the cause of all this trouble."

"How can he be the cause?" Tithonus asked. "He's only a baby."

"Never mind. Everything will be put to rights soon."

The horse was laboring up another steep rise in the ground, and Hippolyta was thinking that they should dismount and walk to ease the climb. But before she could do anything, they reached the top and met with a shock.

The horse suddenly reared up and staggered back, almost tossing both of them to the ground.

"By the goddess!" Hippolyta exclaimed, clinging desperately to the horse's mane.

Tithonus held on tightly to her waist and let out a whoop of alarm.

The ground had suddenly disappeared before them. They were on the very edge of a cliff face that dropped far down to a sunken plain below. And in the center of that plain was a city.

"Arimaspa!" they both cried out.

CHAPTER TWENTY-THREE

ARIMASPA

Hippolyta finally managed to bring the horse back under control and stared down at their discovery. Below them, long, empty streets rayed out beyond the crumbling walls. Nothing seemed to be alive down there; nothing was stirring. Not birds or animals or people.

"Is this it?" Tithonus asked. "Is this Arimaspa?"

"Unless there's another lost city around here," Hippolyta replied.

They got off the horse and cast around for a way down. Tithonus found a steep slope. "There!" he cried out, pointing.

"We'll never make it down that in one piece," Hippolyta said.

They walked the horse along the cliff's edge, and farther on, Hippolyta saw an ancient track that descended at a more agreeable angle. But it was badly rutted and looked barely passable. She pointed.

"*That?*" Tithonus' voice held pure astonishment.

"That," she answered, and slowly headed the horse in the direction of the old road.

Now that Arimaspa lay before them, Hippolyta felt in no hurry to discover its secrets, for the darkest secret of all was her own: Tithonus was to be her sacrifice. His life was the price to be paid for the safety of her people. If he died, they lived.

If he died . . . That thought sat in her chest like a lump of undigested meat, threatening to come back up again anytime she opened her mouth.

So she kept her mouth firmly closed.

The closer they drew to the city, though, the more she was aware of what lay before her. She wanted to tell someone. But the only one with her was the one person she could not tell.

No one else can do what I have to do, she told herself. *No one else can carry this burden for me.*

Tithonus too had fallen silent, but for a different reason: The eerie quiet surrounding them had soaked into his soul.

When they finally got to the city walls, they saw how thoroughly the wooden gate had rotted away. Only the arch was left, yawning emptily before them.

Once, Hippolyta thought, *this wall would have deterred any enemy.* Now she could easily count the places where the stones had collapsed. The city of Arimaspa had no defenses left at all.

Soon they were riding slowly through the empty streets where dilapidated buildings leaned drunkenly against one another.

Hippolyta thought that there was something familiar in this unfamiliar place, but she couldn't place it. No sound of voices or footsteps, no rumble of wagons or crackling of cooking fires. The only noise was the mournful moaning of the wind down the empty streets and the hoofbeats of the horse that had served them so well.

Hippolyta could tell the animal was bone-tired, so she dismounted and had Tithonus do the same. Then, leading the horse, they proceeded farther into the city.

Open doorways and empty windows gaped on every side. Shards of broken pottery and corroded bronze and copperware littered the streets.

Familiar and yet unfamiliar.

"Are there ghosts here?" Tithonus whispered.

Hippolyta startled at the sound of his voice.

"Ghosts . . ." she whispered, as if trying out her voice again. Then she shook her head. "If I were a ghost, I'd rather stay in Tartarus than haunt this dismal place."

As they turned into another street, she suddenly realized why Arimaspa seemed so familiar. The streets of

Themiscyra were laid out along the very same pattern. It was as though an echo of the Amazons' ancient home had remained with them down through the centuries of wandering.

Hippolyta smiled wryly. That meant she knew exactly how to get to the very center of the city, to the Temple of Artemis. "Right here," she said, pointing at one street corner. "Then left."

Tithonus looked at her as if she held magic in her hand. "How do you know that?"

"I just do."

He went silent again, then suddenly blurted out, "I've never lifted a curse before."

"Neither have I," said Hippolyta. "I'm not exactly sure what's going to happen."

Except for one thing, she thought. *One awful thing.*

"I've seen old women making charms," Tithonus said. "Do you think it will be like that? They toss some bones and herbs in a pot and sing over them."

"No," Hippolyta told him. "Not like that." There was a catch in her voice. She blinked three times to keep from crying.

"Don't be afraid," the boy said. "Whatever you have to do, I'll help you." He put his hand on her arm, and much as she wanted to, Hippolyta could not bring herself to pull away from him.

By now they'd reached the main square, and as she'd guessed, there before them stood the Temple of Artemis.

Twice as big as the temple in Themiscyra, it alone seemed to have withstood the siege of time. The edge of the flat roof was intricately carved with scenes of hunting and battle. Huge stone pillars set about with golden vines and gilded laurels framed the entrance.

"Why, it's beautiful!" Tithonus said brightly. "Don't you think so, Hippolyta? Isn't it beautiful?"

Hippolyta put her hand on his shoulder and squeezed hard to shut him up, for suddenly she realized that they were no longer alone. Someone was standing next to one of the pillars and staring down at them.

At first she thought the person standing in the portico was Demonassa, but when Hippolyta looked again, she realized it was someone equally old but quite different from the priestess.

Tithonus saw her staring, followed her line of sight. "Who's that?" he asked.

"Hush!" This time Hippolyta was quite rough with him.

They watched as the old woman walked down the steps toward them. As she got closer, she became younger and younger, the years falling away from her like a series of gossamer veils.

"Artemis," Hippolyta whispered, but not loud enough for the boy to hear.

Artemis nodded approvingly. "The time has come, Amazon. The sacrifice must be made."

Hippolyta swallowed hard and tried to find her

voice. She managed to croak out, "We've faced dangers and hardships together to come here and pay homage to you."

"And it was well done."

"The boy risked his life for me," Hippolyta said. "Isn't that enough?"

There was a flash of annoyance in the goddess's dark eyes. "*Enough?* There is no such thing as *enough* when you deal with the gods. We have a covenant between us, between the gods of Olympus and the race of Amazons, a covenant in which a queen may allow but one of her sons to grow to manhood. That covenant has been broken, so now it must be renewed."

"What's she talking about?" Tithonus interrupted. "Manhood and covenants broken and renewed?"

"Be quiet," Hippolyta warned him. "You're in the presence of the goddess."

Tithonus squinted. "*That* old woman?"

Puzzled, Hippolyta looked again at Artemis, and again she saw only the magnificent young huntress, glowing with youth and power.

The goddess laughed disdainfully. "Did you think he'd know me? How could his childish male eyes be expected to behold my glory? Take up your knife."

"I . . ." Hippolyta hesitated. She looked deep into the goddess's eyes. "I can't lift my dagger against him. We're of the same blood, children of the same mother—"

"There's no need to go on and on," the goddess said

coldly. "If you can't finish what you've started, others will do it for you." She thrust her arm up and pointed.

All at once there was a great rush of wind, so strong both Hippolyta and Tithonus staggered before it. The sound of huge wings beating the air stunned their ears. The sky above them grew heavy and dark.

Looking up, they saw overhead a large vee of winged beasts, much larger than any birds. As the flight came closer, it was clear that these were no ordinary creatures, for each had the golden body and tail of a lion and the proud head, wings, and forelegs of an eagle.

"Gryphons!" Tithonus cried.

Gryphons. Now Hippolyta remembered. They were the same as the beast whose image she'd seen beneath the altar at Themiscyra. And she remembered something else: their sharp talons, their terrible beaks.

"Run!" Tithonus cried. "Gryphons are man-eaters. They'll rip us apart. They'll lap our blood and crack our bones. Run!"

But there was nowhere to run.

Besides, it was too late. The gryphons, a hundred of them at least, had descended upon the city and were even now perching on the rooftops and broken walls on every side of the square, staring down at the children as if waiting, waiting for some kind of awful signal.

CHAPTER TWENTY-FOUR

WINGED VENGEANCE

his is how it was back then," said Artemis, gazing around the square at the creatures and frowning at them. "The gryphons came while Eos, goddess of the dawn, was spreading her rosy mantle across the eastern sky. The air was filled with their warlike screeches and the beating of their awful wings."

Tithonus shuddered, and as if catching the movement from him, Hippolyta shuddered too.

The goddess smiled grimly. "They were sent by my brother, Apollo, sent to mete out his vengeance."

"Vengeance?" Hippolyta asked, glancing over her shoulder at one particularly large gryphon, whose sharp lion ears on the eagle head were twitching back and forth, like a cat when it was ready to pounce. She drew Tithonus closer to her.

Artemis replied, "For the theft of his gold. The gold he uses to fashion his arrows."

"Who—who stole the gold?" Tithonus asked in a voice suddenly made small by fear.

Hippolyta knew that part of the story. "The princes of Arimaspa," she said.

"*Amazons* stole the sun-god's gold?" Tithonus whispered.

The goddess shook her head. "They weren't Amazons then, but the followers of exiled Scythian princes. The same avarice exists in the heart of every *man*."

"I don't want anybody's gold," Tithonus said more loudly.

It was a simple statement, but the goddess turned and glared at him.

Smoothly Hippolyta stepped between them. "How did they steal the gold?"

"The gryphons guarded my brother's mines," Artemis said. At her words the creatures around the square clapped their wings, and the sound was like a hundred swords in battle. "But an oracle informed the Arimaspans that one night in the year the gryphons abandoned their usual vigilance, the night the females laid eggs. So on that very night the princes led their men up the narrow, treacherous paths to Apollo's treasury."

"Ah," Tithonus said. It was such a little sound. Hardly more than a breath. But it made the gryphons in the square clack their beaks. This sound was like the cracking of bones.

Artemis ignored them, continuing with her tale. "They made off with as much gold as they could carry and returned home to a great celebration. But when dawn rose, the gryphons came down from their mountain aerie, filling the sky like a dark storm."

The gryphons in the square moved restlessly on their perches now, making a sound like far-off thunder.

Neither Hippolyta nor Tithonus dared move as Artemis continued. "The men of Arimaspa gathered the women and children into this very temple." She gestured behind her. "The princes ordered them to bolt the door. Then the men drew their swords and prepared to fight. Inside, the women fell to their knees before my altar, praying for mercy and protection."

One of the gryphons in the square cried out then, the sound of lightning after it strikes the ground and sizzles. Hippolyta felt a cold sweat break out on her back.

"The women in the temple could hear the battle raging outside," Artemis said. "The din terrified them. But when silence finally came, it was even more ominous."

Hippolyta nodded. The silence would have frightened her, too.

"At last Lysippe, wife of one of the princes, had the courage to unbolt the door. What a sight greeted their eyes! Everywhere lay the bodies of their men, stabbed and torn by the beaks and talons of the gryphons. The women of Arimaspa wept uncontrollably, tearing their hair and rending their garments. I watched until I could take no more of their weakness."

"*Weakness?*" Hippolyta was appalled. "When is it weakness to cry for the heroic dead?"

"It's weakness if a woman can do *nothing* but weep," Artemis said dismissively. "So I found Lysippe and pulled her to her feet. I picked up her husband's fallen sword and placed it in her hand. 'Enough of this grief,' I told her. 'Enough of weakness and mourning. Rise up, woman, and take your terrible revenge.'"

"Yes," whispered Hippolyta, her left fist clenching tight.

"Lysippe stared at the sword," Artemis said. "There was blood on it from a gryphon her husband had killed. Green blood. I kindled in her heart the anger and the thirst for vengeance she would need."

Artemis watched Hippolyta's face change, grow excited, harden. She smiled, finishing the tale. "One by one, the women each took up a fallen weapon. Sending their children back into the temple, they marched behind their queen into the mountains to the cavern where the gryphons made their nests." Artemis seemed to grow brighter as she spoke, and taller. Her hair rayed out like a great dark sun. "The women took the gryphons by surprise, stabbing and slashing with a ferocity that possessed them like madness."

Hippolyta's hand gripped the haft of her ax. "And did they kill all the beasts?" she cried.

Artemis smiled more broadly still. "Those who could not escape into the sky were slaughtered on their nests. When there were no more adults left to kill, the women turned to smashing the eggs."

"Yes!" Hippolyta cried, and lifted her ax high in the air.

But Artemis' voice was suddenly tempered, as if the fever of the story had left her and all that were needed was the story's moral. "The women abandoned the city, of course. Lysippe promised her followers that they would never again allow themselves to suffer because of man's folly. They sent their male children back to Scythia, then set off for the south to make a new nation of women. They would be all things: farmers, lawmakers, bakers, hunters, but—"

"But above all, warriors." Hippolyta finished for her. This part of the story she knew well.

"Good girl," the goddess said.

"I have heard only some of that tale," Hippolyta said.

"Most of my Amazons have forgotten what happened here," Artemis told her. "But my priestesses remember. Or at least they remember Apollo's decree: If ever an Amazon queen bears a second male child and keeps it, that boy will become ruler of the Amazons and return them to the subjection of men. It may seem a harsh punishment, but my brother wanted vengeance for the slaughter of his gryphons, and I couldn't deny him."

Tithonus stared at the goddess and then at Hippolyta, the truth suddenly dawning on him. "Why *did* you bring me here, Hippolyta?" he asked.

Artemis answered for her. "To die, of course. To be the sacrifice that keeps the Amazons free."

"But I'm not the *second* son," he whispered.

"You are one of two sons, and that is enough," Artemis told him. There was something close to pleasure in her eyes.

At that moment one of the gryphons leaped from its rooftop perch and glided down to the ground. It landed right in front of Tithonus, who fell back from it.

"Come, girl," said Artemis, turning to the temple. "There's sanctuary at my altar." She gestured Hippolyta to follow her. "We'll leave the boy to his fate."

Hippolyta wrenched her eyes from the goddess with great difficulty and watched as the gryphon backed Tithonus toward a far wall with lazy confidence. Its sharp claws clicked on the cracked paving stones, its beak snapped playfully. There was a fluttering and a harsh murmur from above as the other gryphons anticipated the kill.

"Come into the temple," Artemis insisted, mounting the first few steps. "You don't have to watch this."

"Don't believe her," Tithonus yelled, his voice loud

enough to make the gryphon on the ground mantle its wings for a moment. "Don't believe that story of hers. Who do you think told the people of Arimaspa they could steal from Apollo and get away with it?"

His words hit Hippolyta like darts.

He's right, she thought suddenly. *There's some wrongness at the heart of Artemis' story.* But she couldn't think what it could be.

Artemis lifted an arm, and as if that were some signal, the gryphon trailing the boy swept out one of its great wings and knocked him flat on his back. Then it pinned him to the ground with one massive paw.

The goddess smiled a serpent smile, all teeth and no lips, as she watched the creature prepare for the kill.

For an instant Hippolyta saw her again as the old woman, her eyes hardened with years of selfish cruelty.

"Tithonus is right," Hippolyta gasped. "You—you said an oracle told them how to get past the gryphons. But an oracle only speaks for a god—or a goddess. It was *you*, wasn't it, Artemis? It was *you* who sent the Scythians to rob your brother."

"What of it?" snapped the goddess, coming back down the steps and seizing Hippolyta by the arm. "Hadn't Apollo's followers just dishonored one of my shrines in Arcadia? He started the war, and it was time for *his* pride to suffer."

Hippolyta pulled away from the goddess's icy grip. Raising her ax, she ran toward Tithonus.

The gryphon spotted her and reared up, baring its vicious claws. It screamed at her with its lightning-strike voice, and Tithonus used that moment to scramble away.

Then Hippolyta swung her double-headed ax and sliced clean through the beast's feathered throat. It fell to the ground, green blood puddling beneath its body.

At once an earsplitting cry went up from the other gryphons, and they rose into the air as one. The beating of their wings sent a huge wind whipping around the square. Tithonus grabbed hold of Hippolyta's tunic to keep from being blown over.

"I knew you wouldn't leave me, Hippolyta," he gasped.

She didn't answer.

"Come, Hippolyta," Artemis said sternly. "It's not too late. I can still grant you sanctuary. Without my help, you'll be torn to bits, just like the boy." She beckoned toward the temple.

"Not unless Tithonus goes in there as well," Hippolyta answered defiantly.

"Impossible!" The goddess's voice was hard as stone. "Men are not allowed—"

"We live together or die together," said Hippolyta.

"Why?" the goddess demanded.

"Because—because he's my brother. Because there's no reason he should die just for your hurt pride or Apollo's. Either one of you could lift the curse on the

Amazons without any such a sacrifice if you wanted to."

A gryphon dived out of the sky at her, and she lashed out with her ax. She felt its beak crack under the impact before it wheeled away, shrieking in pain.

Tithonus squared his shoulders and called to the goddess, "If you're so keen on sacrifices, why don't *you* lie down under the dagger yourself?" It was the ultimate challenge. "Then you might not be so ready to watch humans die for your sake."

"I *will* watch you die," said Artemis grimly. "Both of you. And enjoy every last bloody moment."

The beating of gryphon wings grew louder as the creatures massed above them for a full-scale attack.

"Together," whispered Tithonus to Hippolyta.

She looked at him and smiled lopsidedly. "Yes, together."

CHAPTER TWENTY-FIVE

JUDGMENT

ippolyta shoved Tithonus behind her and lashed out with her ax. The ax clipped the leg of the closest gryphon and sent it darting up into the sky with a howl of pain. A paw batted the cap from her head as another beast made its strike. Hippolyta ducked. Whirling her ax above her head, she sliced feathers from a passing wing, then cracked another beak.

Meanwhile Tithonus set himself back to back with Hippolyta. He pulled out the knife she'd given him days earlier, and then he too busied himself slashing at their attackers. The screeches, sizzles, and howls of the gryphons were almost deafening, and the breeze whipped up by their wings buffeted the two on every side.

The gryphons renewed their attack, and one managed to slip though the slashing blades, its beak tearing a red stripe down Hippolyta's arm. Another, sensing an advantage, followed the first in and raked its sharp claws across the back of Hippolyta's tunic. At the same time, its heavy wing gave Tithonus such a knock on the head, he saw bright stars.

Still, the two children wouldn't stop fighting. Hippolyta's ax drew blood time after time. And if Tithonus wounded fewer, it was because he was smaller, with a shorter blade, not because his heart was any less stout.

But they could feel themselves growing tired. Muscles ached, and sweat ran down their brows so quickly neither one could see very well.

Hippolyta guessed that death was now very close at hand. *Perhaps,* she thought, *perhaps this is what I deserve.* She'd been only too ready to sacrifice Tithonus a short time ago, and now she would die in a vain effort to save him.

A gryphon landed heavily on her shoulders, forcing her to her knees. *Whom can I pray to now?* Hippolyta thought wildly. Then she thought, *Might the gods not accept me as sacrifice in place of the boy?* She smiled under the weight of the creature atop her, thinking, *Perhaps Tithonus could return to Troy, after all, and carry with him a fond memory of his dead sister.*

From somewhere far away she heard Tithonus cry

out, but whether it was in pain or anger or joy, she couldn't tell. She pitched face downward onto the dirt, thinking that the screeching of the gryphons had changed, too. There was terror in it now as well as triumph and rage.

"Oh, Mother," she whispered through lips as stiff as stone, "wait for me." And she gave herself over to death.

But death did not seem to want her, and she pushed herself back onto her knees, dimly aware that someone was standing over her, fighting off the gryphons in her stead.

Looking up blearily, she saw a black-bearded warrior in bronze armor wielding a wide-bladed sword and fending off the claws of his attackers with a round shield.

"Polemos!"

Had she said his name aloud? She couldn't tell. But for a moment he looked down at her and grinned. Then he focused all his energies on the attacking creatures.

Sunlight broke through the shadow of the circling flock as the gryphons drew back from the Lycian's bloodstained blade. Ten or twelve of them lay dead on the ground by his feet.

Tithonus helped Hippolyta up. His face gleamed with pale horror, but his voice held pure joy. "Look, Hippolyta, it's Polemos. He's come out of nowhere to save us!"

"He always comes out of nowhere," she said.

Breathing hard, she felt as if her chest were on fire, as if her whole body had been beaten with hammers.

"You can call off your pets now, Apollo!" Polemos yelled over the din of the gryphons.

Hippolyta gasped at his tone.

"If I don't," a smooth voice replied, "they'll beat you eventually and eat *your* little pets. You know that, don't you?"

"And how many do you think I'll kill before that happens, Apollo?" Polemos retorted. "A hundred? Two hundred? More?"

Suddenly a tall, bronze-skinned youth, long black curls cascading over his shoulders, appeared from the shadow of a tall building and strode across the square toward them. He was so handsome, Hippolyta had to look away.

"Good question, cousin," Apollo admitted. "Let's not put it to the test today."

He gave a dismissive wave of his hand, and at once the whole flock of gryphons wheeled into the sky, turned toward the mountains, and flew away. With their departure the sun blazed down on the city like the light of a fresh dawn.

"You always were a troublemaker, Ares," the young man drawled to Polemos. "Always interfering in other people's business."

"*Ares?*" Tithonus wrinkled his nose. "The god of war?"

Polemos turned to him, grinning. "Not what you expected?"

So that's how he can appear so suddenly, Hippolyta thought. *And shoot so accurately, and—*

Tithonus chewed his lip and fidgeted nervously. "I always thought you'd be, well, a bit of a bully," he said abashedly.

"That's what the other gods would like you to believe," said Ares, casting a meaningful glance at Apollo.

"You used to bully *me* when I was young," Apollo said.

"That was aeons ago," Ares said. He smiled. "I was just trying to keep you in line."

Hippolyta thought she might have found it amusing if she weren't so tired. If blood and sweat weren't running down her face.

Artemis stomped up to the war god, put her hands on her hips, and fixed him with a belligerent stare. "You've no business here, Ares. Why don't you go back to that armory you call a home?"

"*I* have no business here?" Ares repeated, raising an eyebrow. "Don't the Amazons worship me as well as you, Artemis? Besides, *you* were trying to kill my daughter."

He turned slightly and put a gentle hand on Hippolyta's hair.

"Y-Your daughter?" she stammered.

"Your mother swore never to tell you," said Ares. "She thought it might go to your head if you knew your father was a god." He laughed. "But anyone seeing the three of us together would have guessed. You look nothing like Otrere."

"You look like him!" Tithonus crowed. "I see it now. The dark hair, the crooked smile, the same color—"

"No, I don't!" Hippolyta insisted. But she knew, with sudden conviction, that she did.

"Whether she's your daughter or not, Ares, she's still a mortal and must be bound by our laws," Artemis insisted.

"Half mortal," said Ares. "And this has *nothing* to do with laws. It's all about your empty rivalry with your brother. The two of you have been quarreling for so many centuries, you believe the whole world revolves around your disputes."

Brother and sister, Hippolyta thought. Then she looked over at Tithonus. *We won't quarrel that way,* she promised herself.

But the gods were still arguing.

"Why shouldn't mortals do as we say?" asked Apollo. "Aren't we the gods?"

"Yes, we're the gods, and we've the means to fight our own battles," said Ares. "Let men fight for their own reasons: to defend their truths, to protect those they love—"

"To gain gold or ground or tell someone else how to worship," sneered Apollo.

Artemis folded her arms and glared at Ares. "So you take their side against your fellow immortals."

"I am the warrior's god, after all," said Ares firmly. "Many times mortals are at their worst when they fight, but often they are at their best then, too. Battle displays human courage, determination, willingness to sacrifice for something they value even more than their own lives. Just look at Hippolyta. She was ready to give up her own life in defense of her brother. That's more than either of you two would ever do."

"You're a fool, Ares," Artemis declared, stamping her foot. "Would you have us take lessons from mortals?"

"Who else is there for us to learn from?" said Ares. "Now end this foolishness, and lift your curse from the Amazons."

Brother and sister stared at each other for a long moment, and Hippolyta wondered what would happen. She could feel a bead of cold sweat running down her spine. When the gods decided to do something, humans could only wait and hope.

Then Apollo nodded slowly, and Artemis did likewise, though it was with a sullen look on her pretty face. Each raised a hand in the air, and a bolt of light shot from the space between their fingers, merging above the city. The light arced across the sky like a shooting star flying up to the heavens and then was gone.

"There," said Artemis, scowling. "It's done."

"Now go," Ares ordered them, "back to Delphi or Olympus, I don't care where. See if you can settle your differences without bringing harm to anyone else."

"We'll go," Apollo agreed with a curl of his lip. "But even without us, mortals will still find things to fight over."

"Perhaps," Ares said. "But at least those disputes will be their own. And they'll learn to settle things themselves."

"We'll go for now," Artemis said, leaning toward her cousin. "But we won't promise to stay away."

Apollo nodded and stood close to his sister. A nimbus of gold surrounded them both, as if they were twinned in a womb of light. As the nimbus tightened around them, they seemed to fade into the air until they were just motes of sunlight dancing in the sunlit town square.

Hippolyta and Tithonus both breathed huge sighs of relief, and the boy turned to Ares. "So *you* were Polemos," said Tithonus.

"And before that," Hippolyta added, rubbing a hand through her hair, "you were the old man by the river."

"Yes." Ares nodded. "I was both. We gods change shape as easily as you change your clothes."

"But why did you keep your identity a secret?" asked Tithonus.

"I couldn't interfere directly in your journey," Ares explained. "Father Zeus doesn't allow it."

Hippolyta laughed. "That javelin was pretty direct. And fighting off the gryphons."

"I was simply rebalancing where Apollo and Artemis had already interfered," he said. "The Fates had marked out a particular path for you, and *that* I couldn't change. But I wanted to prepare you, Hippolyta, for what was to come. To teach you how to fight—when and why. Because what you are now, you will be later on. I must say, you've learned both lessons well."

Tithonus shifted from one leg to another. "And me? Did you want to teach me, too?"

Ares shook his head. "You aren't my son, Tithonus. You are your own father's child. And he has taught you."

The boy's face fell. "I don't like what I've learned from him."

Ares patted him on the head. "That's a kind of teaching as well."

Hippolyta felt anger and something else rise like heat in her cheeks. "Why now? Why have you never come to me before?"

"I thought you didn't care who your father was," Tithonus reminded her.

Hippolyta ignored him and pressed Ares. "Did you care so little for me that you never once in thirteen years came to visit?"

"Your thirteen years are but a passing flicker of time to a god," Ares said in a gentle voice. "And it won't be long before you're queen of the Amazons in your own right. Before that time comes, I wanted to know that you would lead them well, not in a spirit of savagery, as Valasca would have it, but with courage and nobility." He undid a belt with a bronze buckle from around his waist.

"Wear this, and all will know you've found the god's favor."

She hefted the belt. "Me? Queen of the Amazons? But why me? My sister Orithya—she's older. Or Melanippe—she's smarter. Or Antiope—everyone loves her." Hippolyta shook her head.

"Read in the remains of this city what happens when a selfish ruler goes head to head with a vengeful god." Ares gestured at the abandoned ruins. "From now on, let the Amazons be free of such folly. You, my daughter, will know that lesson best. Put on the belt."

She thought for a moment about refusing, then remembered how the Amazons could still fall into Valasca's hands. Her mother's voice came to her then, saying, "If Valasca is rid of me, she'll plunge our sisters into years of empty, bloody warfare." Resolutely she tied the belt around her waist. It was heavier than it looked.

Like queenship, she thought.

"I hope my father doesn't bring doom to Troy the way the king of Arimaspa ruined this city," said Tithonus glumly.

"You'll know what to do if he does," Hippolyta said. She slipped the serpent bracelet off her arm and handed it to him. "Let this remind you of your courage on this long journey and recall to you the love your sister bears you."

"And let's worry about one curse at a time," said Ares,

giving the boy a playful slap on the back. "I have a chariot close by that will carry us to Themiscyra faster than you can imagine."

"I can imagine pretty fast," Tithonus said.

"Not too fast," Hippolyta cautioned. "After all, Father, we have a lot of catching up to do along the way."

CHAPTER TWENTY-SIX

AND HOME

Ares' chariot sped homeward with the swiftness of the wind. He could have gotten them to Themiscyra in a single night, but heeding Hippolyta's plea, he went the long way around.

His horses never tired, but knowing his passengers to be mortal, he stopped frequently to let them eat and rest.

Tithonus suspected nothing, but Hippolyta understood that each stop cost them time the god could have easily dismissed. But he remained charming and effortlessly found game to provide them with food. At each meal he regaled them with tales of ancient heroes.

On the second evening, while Tithonus lay wrapped in a blanket sleeping peacefully, Hippolyta asked Ares about her mother and how they had met.

Sitting with his back against a tree, and scratching there like some great cat, Ares spoke. "I was traveling the mortal world and decided to visit the land of the Amazons in the guise of a messenger bringing gifts from King Sagellus of Scythia," he said.

"Why not just travel as yourself?" asked Hippolyta, eagerly leaning into the tale.

He smiled at her. "And what's the fun of that?" he asked. "After so many aeons, *myself* is a boring way to travel."

"Is this"—she pointed at him—"really what you look like then?"

He smiled again and didn't answer, electing instead to finish his story. "I found the young queen Otrere tending a girl who'd been injured during spear practice. After gently washing and binding the wound, she showed the girl how to protect herself, how to fight without lowering her guard."

"Funny," mused Hippolyta, "I can't think of my mother as a fighter."

Ares smiled as he remembered. "Never before had I come upon a woman who so perfectly combined both strength and tenderness in her actions and words. I loved her at once, and while I enjoyed the hospitality of her court, I wooed her with all my heart. Only when I had won her love did I reveal my true nature to her."

"What did she say then?"

Ares grinned. "She laughed. She said she thought a god would be handsomer."

Hippolyta laughed, too. Then she thought of Apollo, whose beauty outshone the sun. And the golden-haired Laomedon. "I'm glad *you're* my father and not Apollo. Or Laomedon," she said. "Beautiful on the outside, but—"

"Eventually Laomedon will try to cheat the gods once too often," said Ares with a frown, "and that will be his downfall."

She glanced over at the sleeping Tithonus, and faint lines appeared on her forehead.

"Don't worry," Ares assured her, putting his hand on her arm. "He will be safe and happy and far away from Troy when his father's downfall happens."

"And when he is king?"

Area shook his head. "He will *never* be king of Troy."

Hippolyta smiled. "That's all right. He doesn't want to be king anyway." She made a strange sound then, half laugh, half sigh. "It's the fighting, you know. He hates it. Though when he had to, he watched my back and never gave up. And kings need to know how to fight. At least kings of Troy."

"There will be no peace for Troy, that is certain," said Ares. "But one day Trojans and Amazons will fight side by side as allies and friends, and that will be because of you."

"I'm glad," Hippolyta told him. "I should like to see Dares again, at least, to thank him for his kindness."

"I have told you more than I should," Ares said.

Hippolyta heard the caution in his voice. "Bedtime stories, really. Father to daughter." She leaned over and kissed him on the brow. "Good night."

Over the remaining three days of the journey Tithonus became his old talkative self once more. He plied Ares with questions about the other gods and told his own stories of life in Troy.

Hippolyta couldn't help being amused at seeing her father strain to maintain his patience with the continual chatter, and she was sure that the more Tithonus talked, the more Ares urged his horses to greater speed.

When they entered the country of the Amazons at last, Hippolyta was relieved to see that things were back to normal: workers in the fields and armed riders upon the roads. When one of the patrols blocked their way, Ares addressed them imperiously. "I am Polemos, envoy of King Sagellus of Scythia," he announced in a booming voice. "I am escorting the princess Hippolyta, daughter of Otrere, back to Themiscyra."

At once the warriors drew aside and let them pass.

"Why didn't you tell them who you really are?" asked Tithonus.

"When you tell people you're a god," Ares explained, "either they take you for a madman and try to lock you up, or they won't let you pass without accepting gifts and sacrifices. Believe me, it's a lot simpler just to lie in a loud voice."

That's not what he told me, Hippolyta thought, remembering how Ares had said that traveling simply as himself was boring. She wondered where the real truth of it lay. *Probably somewhere in between*, she thought. Then she realized that was a good definition of a god's truth.

As they drew closer to Themiscyra, most of the Amazons they passed recognized Hippolyta and called out to her. She pleaded with Ares to stop the chariot so she could speak to them, to ask them about her mother and her sisters.

"We'll be there soon enough," he answered.

And with a flick of the reins he redoubled the speed of his horses so that the countryside flew by like a river in torrent. When they finally pulled up before the walls of the city, Hippolyta had to gasp for breath.

Ares gestured for the two children to step down from the chariot.

"But aren't you coming in with us?" Hippolyta asked.

Ares shook his head. "My business lies elsewhere."

"But Mother . . . don't you want to see her?"

A faraway look passed briefly across Ares' rugged face. "I can see her as clearly now as the day when first I loved her. But that is in the past and must remain so. Never encourage a god to interfere in your life." He laughed. "Actually, we don't need much prompting."

"Will I see you again?"

"You don't need to. You don't need any of the gods. You are free to follow your own path now."

"What about me?" Tithonus piped up.

"That is for you to decide," said Ares. "I can take you back to Troy or leave you here. The choice is yours."

"Choice?" Hippolyta looked at Ares strangely, remembering what he'd said about Tithonus' future. There was no choice built into that.

As if reading her mind, Ares leaned down across the chariot's side and said, "There are many different paths to one's destiny. Do not confuse journey's end with the journey."

"Demonassa always said that the gods speak in riddles and not straight on."

"I *am* speaking straight on," Ares told her. "You are not listening." He stood up again, looking very stern.

And like a god, not like a father, thought Hippolyta, though for her the two were equally distant.

Ares held out his hand, and Hippolyta took it, one warrior to another.

As if he hadn't heard their conversation, Tithonus looked at Hippolyta and bit his lip. "You promised me I would meet my mother. Last time didn't count. She was—she was not herself."

Even now that they were safe, Hippolyta felt a twinge of guilt over how she had deceived Tithonus. "If you come with me into the city now, the Amazons will give you an escort back to Troy later."

He nodded shyly, and she took his hand.

Ares let out a sudden mighty yell. At once his horses wheeled around and bolted off across the countryside, leaving a trail of dust hanging in the air to mark their passage.

Only after the sound of that yell had faded did Hippolyta turn and pull Tithonus through the city gates, smiling faintly. She didn't look back again.

No sooner were they inside the city walls than an escort of Amazons formed around them to lead them to the square before the Temple of Artemis.

There, on a solid wooden throne, Otrere was dispensing justice, her daughters on one side, Demonassa and her acolytes on the other. Behind them a company of armed warriors stood, with hawk-faced Valasca scowling at their fore.

When they saw Hippolyta, Antiope and Melanippe rushed up to hug her. Orithya welcomed her too with a nod.

Then Queen Otrere opened her arms, and Hippolyta rushed into them, burying her face in her mother's neck, that sweet place where the skin was soft and smelled of spring flowers.

Hippolyta felt overwhelmed, not by grief but by something else. *Joy? Relief?* She didn't know. She wept.

"Don't cry, daughter," her mother said, pushing her gently away. "The time of weeping is over. The grief that overwhelmed us all has disappeared like a passing shower." But as she said this, she too wept.

"There's much work to do after all those days of weeping and wailing," said Demonassa, stepping forward to add her welcome. "Crops and animals have been neglected, and the whole city is in shambles."

"But you're queen again?" Hippolyta asked her mother. "I was prepared to—"

Otrere nodded. "The goddess herself appeared in our midst. She told us that the curse was lifted forever and that there would be no more sacrifice of children, not now or in the future."

Behind her, Hippolyta heard the sound of a heavy sigh. She knew that sound. It was Tithonus.

Tithonus. She had to introduce him!

But Demonassa was speaking, so Hippolyta held her tongue. Hadn't her father said there were many paths to one's destination? She would wait for the explanations to be over.

"Artemis—blessed be—told us that you had fulfilled the quest she had given you to seek out the lost city of Arimaspa," the priestess was saying. "And that there you fought with the courage of a true Amazon."

"And look what the goddess left behind," Antiope

added excitedly. She pointed her little finger at the lintel over the door of the temple. A carving had been placed there, wrought in exquisite detail. It was Hippolyta herself, standing over Tithonus and fighting off the gryphons with her ax.

"When I saw this, I knew I had been right to defy a cruel law," said Otrere, "and I knew that you understood why I did it."

"Yes, I do," Hippolyta agreed. "And I've brought a surprise back with me: your oldest son, Tithonus."

Tithonus stepped forward, a bit bashfully, intimidated by the crowd of Amazons who pressed in on every side. Otrere stood up, took a step toward him, then wrapped her arms around him.

A murmur of surprise passed through the square.

Otrere looked around, one arm still resting on her son's shoulder. "This is something we all must learn," she said. "It was not love for our sons that brought a curse upon us. It was the vengeful ways of the past, which we will follow no longer."

She stared hard at Valasca, who slowly lowered her head. "It will be as you say, Otrere," the warrior queen conceded, "but I shall not abandon my task of protecting our people."

"Protect our people by all means," said Otrere, "but not by making war upon our neighbors for no reason other than your desire for battle."

It was clear from the way the crowd listened to her

that Otrere's authority over the Amazons had been fully restored. Valasca and her small band of followers turned away and left the square. Only Molpadia, her face screwed up in anger, looked back.

"Come, Tithonus," said Otrere with a smile, "let's go into the palace, where you and your sister can tell me all about your adventures."

The boy's face lit up. "Oh, yes, there's lots to tell," he said.

Hippolyta laughed. "I hope you don't have much else to do today, Mother. This could take quite some time."

WHAT IS TRUE ABOUT THIS STORY?

Did the Heroic Age, the Age of Heroes, really exist?

Yes and no.

No, there was not a time when the gods took part in human battles, nor were there gryphons flying about deserted cities or sea monsters scouring the countryside because of a curse.

But yes, there was once a rich and powerful civilization in Greece that we call Mycenae, where each city was a separate state with its own king but where the people were united by a single language. There was a thriving culture too, many days' ride to the east near the Black

Sea (which was then called the Euxine Sea), though there is no evidence of the city we call Themiscyra or a nation of women.

However, in that same time period there was a real Troy. Legend has it that in a continuing attempt to get rid of the sea monster, King Laomedon tied his own daughter, Hermione, to the rock as a sacrifice. Hercules showed up in his travels and offered to kill the monster and save the girl. All he wanted in exchange was a set of fabulous horses that Laomedon owned. Laomedon agreed, but when Hercules did the deed, Laomedon refused to pay him. Hercules proceeded on with his journey but returned a few years later and captured Troy. He killed Laomedon and all his sons except Tithonus, who had long ago disappeared into Ethiopia, some said as consort to the goddess of the dawn, and Podarces. Hermione ransomed her brother Podarces, who thereafter was known as Priam, which means "ransomed." When the Trojan War began, a force of Amazons, led by Queen Penthesilea, came to the aid of the Trojans under King Priam. During the long war the Amazon queen and her followers were all slain, as was King Priam and his son, Hector. There was a real Troy and a real war, but the rest is probably legend.

Folk stories about a tribe of warrior women called Amazons living in the area of the Caucasus (then called the Rhipaean Mountains) were told and retold by the Greeks. The foundation of many towns—Smyrna,

Ephesus, Paphos among them—is attributed to them. Legends said that two rebel Scythian princes had founded a town that became the birthplace of the Amazon race. A number of famous heroes—like Bellerophon, who tamed the flying horse Pegasus, and even the mighty Hercules—were said to have fought against the Amazons. In fact it is related that one of Hercules' famous twelve labors was to bring back the girdle (belt) belonging to the Amazon queen Hippolyta, a belt reputedly given to her by her father, Ares, the god of war. We know from one version of these tales that Hippolyta and her sister Melanippe were killed in the fight. In other versions, only Melanippe dies. And in the stories about Theseus, the great hero who slew the Gorgon Medusa, there is one in which he carries off Antiope, the peacemaker, to be his bride. Hippolyta then tracks them down and lays siege to his city. Antiope and Molpadia both die in that battle, and Hippolyta supposedly retires to the city of Megara, where she dies some time later of grief.

Stories. Legends. Tales.

But a woman—even a mythic hero—must have a childhood and adolescence that foretell her future deeds. We know little about the Amazon queen called Hippolyta beside the stories of her battles with Bellerophon, Hercules, and Theseus. We know from these stories only that she was heroic, brave, headstrong, loyal to her family, and beloved as a great leader.

Archaeologists and folklorists tell us more. The

Amazons were presumably the founders of the town of Themiscyra in a country on the River Thermodon. Their principal pursuits were hunting and agriculture. They were ruled by two queens, one for defense and one for domestic affairs. When the Amazons rode to war, they carried ivy-shaped shields and double-bladed battle-axes. But they were not the single-minded warriors that so many tales would have us believe. They also produced artistic treasures that were sought after by many of their trading neighbors.

For some four hundred years (1000–600 B.C.), they ruled parts of Asia Minor along the shores of the Black Sea. But Plutarch (among others) reported that the Amazons invaded Athens. History mixing with fiction.

One of the most persistent beliefs about the Amazons was that they surgically removed their right breasts, in order to make it easier to draw the bow and throw the javelin. But scholars no longer believe this, as there is no evidence in Greek art that shows the Amazons as mutilated women. Usually they are shown on horseback, often bare-breasted, sometimes in Scythian dress—a tight fur tunic, a cloak of many folds, a fur cap. However, there is an even more persistent belief: that the Amazons had children with men from surrounding tribes, or with their own male captives or slaves, and kept only the daughters of those unions, returning any sons to the tribe of origin or sometimes killing or crippling the boys. Is it true? Is any of it true?

We can only guess. That is what a historical fantasy story is, after all, a well-told guess.

We have taken the Hippolyta of the legends and tales and projected her backward, using what archaeologists have told us about the civilization she would have inhabited if she had been a real young woman.

Or a young hero.